WHAT WE DID ON OUR HOLIDAYS

FELICITY McCALL

Colmcille
Press

Published July 2025 by
Colmcille Press, Ráth Mór Centre, Derry BT48 0LZ
Managing Editor Garbhán Downey
www.colmcillepress.com
Layout and design by Joe McAllister

© Felicity McCall/Colmcille Press

ISBN 978 1 914009 51 8

Colmcille Press gratefully acknowledges the support of Creggan Enterprises Limited. The author also thanks the Arts Council of Northern Ireland and Derry City and Strabane District Council for their support.

  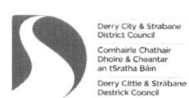

The moral rights of the author have been asserted in accordance with the Copyright, Designs and Patents Act, 1998.

A CIP copy for this book is available from the National Library of Ireland and the British Library.

All rights reserved. No part of this publication may be reproduced or transmitted in any form or by any means, electronic or mechanical, including photocopy, recording, or any information storage or retrieval system, without permission in writing from the publisher. The book is sold subject to the condition that it shall not, by way of trade or otherwise, be lent, re-sold or otherwise circulated without the publisher's prior consent in any form of binding or cover other than that in which it is published and without a similar condition including this condition being imposed on the subsequent purchaser.

What We Did on Our Holidays

My cotton swimsuit is sodden with salt water, Mammy, and caked with sand, sand that clings to the troughs between each stinging row of shirring elastic. It's blue, with little yellow flowers patterning it and straps that tie behind my neck. I am so excited when you twirl me in front of the dressing-table mirror in yours and Da's big bedroom. It fits. It has been far down the gaberdine kit bag stashed on the top shelf of the wardrobe since before I can remember, when my sister was the age I am now. Three. Three-coming-four. Three is fragmented memory of a card with a panda playing a drum, of sandwiches made from thick white bread and mushy tomato. My sister and her friends, pouring brown lemonade from the blue plastic teapot in the dolls' tea set that is now, magically, mine. The plastic makes everything taste strange. I test it with my teeth. It is hard. My teeth leave little pockmarks on the rim of the cup. Three is knowing you are three. And wanting to remember. And good.

The swimsuit is good, too, as it means I am big enough to go to the unknown territory you love, The Seaside. Your best stories are about the little girl who went to the seaside with her daddy. That little girl is you. You didn't have a mummy. Your daddy couldn't walk, so a nurse in a white starched apron, with a funny big white head dress, used to push him along the promenade. You would skip alongside him, and sometimes he would pull you on to his lap, if your chubby little legs were tired – he always knew – and the nurse would push you both. He would watch while you filled your red tin bucket with soft damp sand, patting into place, upending it to make a castle that always crumbled, digging a moat round it and waiting to see if the tide would fill it. Scavenging for opalescent white shells to stud into the crumbling mound. Draping it with strands of slimy green seaweed. Not being sad when the incoming tide took it away, and you had to leave the beach, quickly, quickly. Because nothing lasts forever, your daddy says, but you have the day safe in your heart where no one can take it from you.

After, you'd make your way back along the promenade and into the cafe. Downstairs for teas and ice creams, upstairs for the big feeds. You are always downstairs. The table is round and has a shiny, mottled green and white marble top. Its twisted legs, and the chairs, are wrought iron. Cold beneath your thighs. The marble is so smooth, so lovely to stroke. Exotic birds and blossoms adorn the wallpaper. A girl in a black dress with a white apron – tiny, frilly, not like the nurse's – takes your order. You struggled to be patient until she returns with a tray laden with dimpled glass dishes scooped to the rim with glistening, soft ivory ice cream, with raspberry sauce dribbled over the top and two wafers poking out of it at a jaunty angle. You smile because the grown-ups are having ice cream, too, as well as pots of tea. The spoon is long, unwieldy, as you stir the melting dish of pink and white mottled sweetness. Your daddy smiles, gentleness lighting his eyes, and holds your sticky hand. And the ice cream and the seaside and daddy are the best thing ever.

How many days were there like this, fused into one perfect memory?

And while the ice cream and the red tin bucket and the nurse and your daddy are long gone, the joy has stayed safe in your heart. Like your daddy said it would. Like he promised.

It is my favourite story when you lift me from the tin bath in front of the stove and wrap me in the biggest towel and gently, always gently, rub dry my hair. Better than the one about how you ran away to London, where there was a war on and how you told fibs about your age and lived in a hostel with lots of English girls who couldn't cook and were woefully undomesticated. Better than the one about how the Irish airman she had been writing to rang the hostel to say he was on leave and asked to visit you. How the girls pooled their dresses, and you chose the prettiest. That is a big people's story, a love story.

But I never tire of hearing about the seaside. And now I am here and I am doing my best not to cry because whatever I imagined it is nothing like the seaside of the story. You say it is the same seaside, and look so happy, and Daddy squeezes your hand, and you smile. You are so happy that I sense I must not cry.

How can it be? The wet elastic is cutting into my plump little legs, leaving raw red itchy welts. The sky is grey, foreboding, and I am shivering. Daddy takes me to the edge of the water and guides me into the shallow waves. He shows me how to count to three, then hunker down into the water, up and down till I am warmer. To splash the chilly water on my chest, to get it over with. Then after what seems a long, long time, he leads me back across the interminable stretch of sand that is rough underfoot and clings to the soles of my feet, cakes between my toes. The tide is going out, and it has left rippled ridges in the sand that hurt, too. Finally, I reach you and the picnic bag. You have brought a big bag. You need one. From its depths you pull the huge striped towel and wrap me in it, wriggling me out of the swimsuit, asking if I enjoyed my first dip. I press my lips firmly together. I mustn't cry. Then you dress me, but the gritty sand clings beneath my vest and shorts; it bites into me through my blue plastic sandals, and the metal buckle rubs the soft flesh of my chubby little feet until it draws blood.

You are telling the seaside story, but I do not hear it. You tell it as you spread the tarpaulin on the sand dunes, as you pour steaming black tea from the tartan flask into the lid, lacing it with lukewarm milk from a medicine bottle. You untwist the packet of sugar and stir in two heaped spoons, as it's for me. I wrap my hands round it and pull it close to me to warm my chest. You scold yourself for not having brought my anorak.

There are tomato sandwiches but my hands are numb and I drop mine. Now it is caked with sand too, like my feet and fingers and tummy. I push it away, even though it is a waste and you hate waste. There are Marie biscuits that have broken in the packet, so I am allowed to dunk them and suck out the hot, sweet tea. I start to feel warmer. I can have as many as I want as you say there's no point in taking them home. You screw up the wrapper and drop it into the big straw bag. You pull out a squashed up blue and white thing. Daddy puts it to his lips, screws up his face in concentration and blows. It is a big, soft, floppy ball called a beach ball and we play Piggy in the Middle with you and Da throwing the ball nice and low to give me a chance. I'm not cold any more. I am laughing. The sky darkens and Daddy hoists me up on to his shoulders while you shake the tarpaulin, folds it on top of the big straw bag and we head back towards the car.

And then we drive to the promenade and we find the cafe and you are sure it is the same one, only the wallpaper has been replaced by laminated panelling, the marble table by white plastic. We sit downstairs. There is no sign of the young waitress so Daddy goes to the counter and returns with a tray laden with three plates of chips and a pot of tea. The salt cellar has one big hole and Daddy warns me to be careful or I'll spoil my chips. There is a plastic bottle of brown malt vinegar. There is a red plastic tomato that squeezes red sauce, and I squeeze out far too much. And after, there is ice cream in a cone, not a dish, but with raspberry squirted on top and wrapped in greaseproof paper and it melts over my hand as I eat it walking back to the car while you and Da hold hands. Drowsing in the back seat, I feel warm and full and happy. I wish would tell the seaside story all over again, now I am listening. Then I realise I have one of my own now, that no one can take away. That I can keep in my heart forever.

I am so glad I didn't cry and you are right, as she always are, and The Seaside is the best place in the world

* * * *

The beloved man with the cold hands and the warm heart is gone now. So is the little girl.

But today, Mammy and I are going to the seaside.

I'm taking a big bag. I'll need it. Hooded rain jacket. Battery pack for my phone. Notebook and pen. Makeup bag, though the chances of five minutes' peace in the Ladies are, frankly, nil. Bottle of water. A couple of tangerines and a box of chopped melon. They're for me as lunch has been ordered for us all and it may be the sort of institutional fare I choose to avoid.

The nurses will have their own capacious bag. Nappies, bibs, emergency medication, spare clothes, extra layers. Wet wipes and tissues. Cartons of juice drinks with a straw.

But Mammy and I are going to the seaside, the same seaside. I am so excited on her behalf when I hear she is well enough to be included in the outing – provided I am there, too. I count myself privileged.

We wait outside while the minibus is loaded with its fragile passengers. We will be among the last to get on as Mammy's wheelchair has to be bolted to the floor. She can only be moved by hoist. She has forgotten what her legs are for. She has forgotten most things. I had thought my heart would break the day she forgot me. It broke the day she forgot my da. Not just his name, but every memory built over more than sixty inseparable years. She is getting restless. I tell her again that we are going to the seaside. She smiles. Wherever Alzheimer's has taken her, I am so glad that it seems to be a happy place.

I am so inexpressibly grateful that we are getting this day of unlooked-for happiness. A last visit to the sea. Together. As the ocean comes into view, I search her face for any flicker of recognition. I lean across to speak loudly into her good ear, telling her that we're nearly there, not long now. She has little patience. Is it death she is hurrying towards? She may or may not hear, she may or may not process what I am saying. Still, she smiles.

The bus pulls in on the promenade. I look around for any sign of a care home, but no, we are going to a regular restaurant. The staff have reserved half of the ground floor for our party. There is fish and chips, or chicken and mash. The staff have chosen chicken and mash for Mammy. The mushy mixture she pushes away. I order fish and chips for myself and her eyes twinkle as I surreptitiously break up chips and put them on her plate, cut off small chunks of crispy golden batter. Her enthusiastic appetite sets her apart, causes comment. The bar is open and I get her a white wine and she clutches the fragile stem and sips it appreciatively.

I reminisce about the seaside, how she and Da took me there, how we took my daughter in turn. How a nurse wheeled her own daddy along the promenade as she skipped behind him.

"The wallpaper was different."

The table falls silent.

"The wallpaper was different," she announces, confidently. "None of this wooden stuff. It was proper wallpaper. And the big feeds were upstairs."

"But your daddy couldn't get upstairs because he was in a wheelchair," I prompt.

"We had our ice cream down here," she continues, "and a girl like that one brought it to our table – like they did there now."

"You're getting your ice creams in a wee while," one of the nurses promises. "But first we're going to sit outside."

I buy a second glass of wine while she is wheeled outside, and pull up a chair beside her. She takes my hand. It is a truly beautiful day, not too hot, the sea and sky a rich, clear blue. The sun warms us.

We sit in companionable silence. There is no need for words. Her eyes follow the roll and crash of the waves, and she smiles. With her mouth and her eyes. And, I hope, her heart. I feel a huge swell of unconditional love for this remarkable woman who gave life to me.

Tears well up as I hold her hand tighter.

"That's new. And I think it was over here."

The cafe? Somewhere she stayed? It doesn't matter.

A nurse who overhears us, marvelling at this sudden recall, says that when we get back, she will search the Internet for old photos of the area in the 1920s and print off a selection. I readily agree, knowing that she will not find the catalyst on a printed page. It is here, in the salty tang of the sea air and warmth of the June sunshine, in the crispy golden batter and the ice cream which has just arrived and, joyfully, has raspberry sauce on top. It's in a little waxed dish, not a cone, and the spoon is small and plastic.

She grins. And I wish I could hold this moment forever. I wish her life could end here, now. I wish she could avoid the painfully slow path of deterioration that lies ahead. It is so undeserved. I wish I had that power.

I take her hands to wipe away the stickiness. They are cold.

"*Cold hands, warm heart,*" I say to see if she reacts. She smiles.

"It's changed."

"It must have. It's been ninety years since you first came here," I joke.

"The wallpaper was different."

There is a memory of the mischievous three-year-old's smile flickering across worn features and sagging skin.

Mammy will not remember tomorrow. She will not remember by the time we get back to the home. She is tired. Her eyelids droop. She will sleep away the journey.

My eyes roam the promenade. Maybe, somewhere, I imagine I might glimpse the ghost of the dignified man being wheeled along the promenade while the little girl he can no longer look after, who is his life, skips along beside him, swinging a red tin bucket, and laughs because the seaside is the best place in the world.

Human life must end and buildings crumble but there will

always be sunshine, and frothy waves, and fish and chips and ice cream, and the vital pulse of existence. In that moment, I know that the world is unbelievably good and I will hold this memory within my heart forever.

Mammy looks at her watch. She cannot tell the time now, but habits remain. She will thank everyone for taking her out and say she had a lovely time. Manners are for life.

"I think we should get going now."

Always, now, impatient.

"We have to wait for the bus," I remind her gently, but of course she has no idea how we got here or where we are going back to.

I don't want to leave. I don't want this magical day to end. But she's right – it is time.

Her gaze remains fixed on the sea, and wherever she has gone to, it is good. I have no need to share it. It would be an intrusion.

She is still looking back at the shore as she is pushed towards the bus.

"So, was it all changed?" the nurse asks her.

Clouded eyes, once so vividly green, meet the nurse's and then turn to meet mine.

"It hasn't changed. The sea."

The sea never changes.

Reading the Kerbstones

The taxi stops at the lights. In the back, Ellen is reading the shopfronts: a bookies, two boarded-up premises, a Chinese takeaway, a charity shop with an ugly-looking plastic toy pram on the pavement outside, an off-licence, a home bakery advertising Belfast Baps, flies hovering over sugar sparkled doughnuts filled with artificial cream on the counter. *The mainstays of life in an area like this,* she thinks, and immediately chides herself. Generational poverty is endemic; how dare she judge these streets, not so very different from home?

But they are.

The graffiti is different. The flags on the lampposts are different. The torn political posters are different. The kerbstones are different.

She tries to read the writing on the faded tattoo on the driver's forearm. Ex-military or ex-prisoner? The legend will tell her.

And soon, or so Eimear has reassured her, they will cross an invisible line and the streets will become more prosperous, the flags will recede, the kerbstones return to uniform dull grey. Not what you'd call a salubrious area, but one, Eimear says excitedly, that's on the up, where young professionals, the Children of the Peace, struggling to get on the mortgage ladder, are buying up the affordable doer-upper terraced houses left vacant by the death of the adults of the Conflict. Things are changing, she insists, for these aspirational young who know little and care less about their colleagues' and neighbours' background. Who constitute the fastest growing section of society – the Others.

But they do know, Ellen thinks. *They must do. The clues are always there. Names, schools, pronunciations.* Say nothing. She can still hear Robbie's snort of derision, see her daughter's censorious glare, when she'd asked if it was a *mixed area.*

The lights change and they're off again, the driver tooting to acknowledge a fellow taxi man driving in the opposite direction. Ellen hasn't attempted conversation beyond a vague 'the North West' when he'd enquired where she'd got the train from. She didn't elaborate. Say nothing.

But before they transition this imaginary line in the road, it catches her unawares. A cracked blue laminate sign, an open doorway, just as it had been – what? – thirty, thirty-five years ago? And suddenly Ellen knows the name of the road they are in and struggles to focus as her heart pounds, her stomach contracts, and she finds herself dragged back into a long-buried memory.

The driver has spoken, but she has no idea what he has said.

"Fine, thanks," she mutters, hoping it is the required response. It is also a barefaced lie. She is not fine, She is twenty-two again, alone, and very, very frightened..

* * * *

The taxi drops her at the end of the terraced street. Grey kerbstones, no flags, no graffiti that she can see. Parked cars on both sides, leaving the narrowest gap between them. Streets like this were built long before it was imagined their occupants could own such a thing as a car. She can see the 'For Sale' sign on the left, about a third of the way up. As she approaches, she notices the front door is open, and she catches the sound of voices echoing round the empty rooms – Eimear, Robbie and what must be the estate agent. She taps on the door and walks ahead into a surprisingly light and spacious knocked through lounge/dining room. 1930s art déco fireplace, bay window. She knows at once why Eimear has fallen in love with it. It is every terrace house she has ever called home – granny and grandad's house, the home they had built together, even Eimear's student flat had been part of a Victorian terrace across the city in an area so gentrified now that no young couple could consider buying there. These houses had been her security: Ellen is touched by this continuity of affection – not for Eimear the anonymity of a purpose-built suburban semi with a choice of bathroom and kitchen fittings and a guaranteed mortgage.

Ellen smiles, and entering from the kitchen, Eimear reflects that smile and is pleased.

"You made it in time! See, Mammy. I knew you'd like it. It's lovely, isn't it?"

"Not that we're making an offer today," Robbie remarks pointedly to the estate agent.

"But this is far and away the best of any we've looked at," Eimear interjects, and he nods in agreement.

Ellen recognises her impetuous child. They will make a bid.

She follows them round: a bathroom with black and white chequered period tiles that she loves and Eimear wants replaced; two double bedrooms with floorboards that can easily be varnished; and, above, a tiny attic room for a study, guests, whatever.

A Granny flat? It would be a poor joke; Ellen will never sound needy. And Granny is a pretentious assumption, as non-PC as Mother of the Bride. Anyway, Ellen thinks, the price of houses nowadays they'll both need to be working for a good few years before they even think about childcare costs. If. If they consider childcare costs.

City gas, double glazing. Insulations, damp proof certificate. Their surveyor is happy. Immediate occupancy. Ellen feels herself relax, infected by their barely concealed enthusiasm. Yes, this could be home.

In the cafe on the corner, Eimear is too animated to eat.

"Mammy!"

"Sorry, love."

"Tune in, will you? I said, we're putting on a definite offer of ninety-five and the agent says as it's a probate sale she thinks they'll accept. They want it all done and dusted quickly. None of them live in Ireland any more. We could go to £115k but, like, we'd rather not."

"That twenty k would cover the legal fees and moving, get us a new kitchen, well, new doors on the units at least, and the bathroom re-tiled," Robbie adds.

They're a polished double act, Ellen thinks. They work well together.

"The only other bidder we know of has dropped out. I think they were investors looking for a buy to let and wanting a bargain so they've moved on," Eimear adds.

Ellen pulls herself together. *Focus.* Focus on today. It is, as they say, a lovely house. Or will be.

"I'm glad they kept the fireplaces," she adds, "and everyone tells me the gas is very economic."

"We'll get it put in for you, Ma, when you're a pensioner," Eimear jokes and they all laugh.

It won't be long though.

Waiting at the station, Ellen rubs her instep and looks forward to taking off her shoes off in the carriage, if she can get a table for discretion. She had dressed reasonably smartly, skirt and heels, not anticipating a whistle-stop walking tour of the area, or *the village* as the youngsters insist on calling it. A wealth of coffee shops, all with vegan options; an eco refill store for everything from soaps to fair trade coffee; a greengrocer's like she hadn't seen since her childhood, with a striped awning and a pavement display of glossy cucumbers, apples, plump strawberries, earthy new potatoes; an ice cream parlour where she'd winced at the price of the sundaes. Nearly eight quid each. How did anyone manage to treat a family? Sewing alterations – no one had a sewing machine any more; a traditional barber complete with red and white pole. A little newsagent. A charity shop – she was definitely coming back to browse – the more prosperous the area, the better quality the goods. No pubs, they pointed out, just a couple of licensed restaurants, no bookies, no pound shops, no pawn. Window boxes, cafe gardens where parents sat sipping Lattes while their children ran round sucking organic juice cartons. Charming might be a word. Pretentious? Aspirational, rather, with prices that reflected it. Safe. Anonymously safe.

"Nobody cares what you are here," Eimear had said, knowing her mother too well. "Nobody knows or cares."

Your name might be a clue, Ellen had thought, but then, whose fault was that? She had loved the name, the legend, it was linked in her mind to neither creed nor politics. Cu Chulainn's wife, wooed by solving riddles, won by deeds of valour. A strong woman. No pushover. Like her birth wish for her daughter. But, she knew, it was perceptions that mattered.

She knew too many who had belonged nowhere, disowned by both tribes, and had to make a new life across the water in the anonymity of Manchester or Coventry. Love across the barricades was the stuff of teenage romances written by authors who had never had to live it. There was nothing romantic about it.

So where in this unfamiliar city would she have chosen for them? They had explained, patiently at first, that the university quarter, which was all she knew, was way beyond their budget. So was the South. The North had some good doer-uppers too, but mostly n in need of major work if they were in their price range, and they had neither expertise nor time. They had friends moving into the East, friends of many traditions or none. They could sell for a profit, upsize in a few years.

"Mammy, would you, for the love of God, stop looking at the pavements! Do you think I don't notice the wee sideways glances? You need to chill."

The young would never fully understand. Perhaps that was a good thing. Perhaps that was something she should be proud of. These Children of the Peace, now young adults, counted among the fastest growing section of society – the Others. Refusing to be defined by the perception of what they had been born into. If there was another census, experts predicted more than half of the population would identify as Other, rising with every succeeding generation until, thought Ellen, we are all gone. She found that strangely comforting.

And what a horrible term 'Other' was, implying different, alien, outsider. Surely there was something better? Toying with various ideas – inclusive? Open? – she drifted off, and in that uneasy sleep came the nightmare, as surely as she had known it would the instant she saw that doorway. It had caught her unawares, that was all. She'd had the counselling, was long since free of any medication. It had been taken out of its memory box, revisited, shared, worked through with a wise and patient professional over weeks and months so painful she chose not to dwell on them. And it had worked. Most of the time.

PTSD? Surely that had become shorthand for anyone who'd had a bad experience during the Conflict and, from what Ellen knows, there are very few people who hadn't. She's nothing out of the ordinary. Ellen had never gone for a formal diagnosis. What good might it have done? She didn't want a claim, a disability pension. That was ridiculous,when you saw people round you in wheelchairs, or lost to the numbing effects of prescription drugs, broken souls dead before their time.

She wakes up abruptly in the crowded carriage, shivering, afraid she'd called out, disgraced herself in front of her fellow travellers. She glances round. No one seems to have noticed anything untoward. Ellen takes out her paperback, and buries her face in it, her focus far from the unread pages in front of her.

It is always the same dream that had once been a reality. She had been twenty-two, far younger than Eimear is now, her job at the time taking her across a city in the grip of sectarian conflict. She had left a meeting at a community centre as dusk was falling. Somehow, as she was gathering her things, the group leaders who were to arrange her transport back to work had melted away, leaving only the taciturn caretaker to hurry her out of the building and lock up. When she'd asked if she could ring for a taxi, he had shaken his head and pointed to his watch. Outside, she'd looked round for anyone from the meeting, anyone she might ask for directions. Walking away through the rain in what she hoped was the direction of the City Centre with its familiar lights, shops and taxi ranks, she was aware of the flags flying from lampposts, the graffiti, the wall murals, the painted kerbstones warning her she was far from home. There were no public call boxes. Even if she rang her usual taxi firm, would she be able to describe where she was? Youths with hoodies obscuring their faces, or bomber jackets and tartan scarves, stood hunched in doorways, smoking and drinking cans of lager. Was it her imagination or did she feel eyes boring into her, identifying her as born to an alien tribe – in their eyes, an enemy?

Then she'd seen a taxi rank, no door, open to the elements. Another huddle of purposeless youths leaning on the chipboard counter or slumped on the bench inside the door. Ellen had summoned her courage and braved the tangible hostility to ask for a cab.

"Name?" the dispatcher was sizing her up, and she knew it.

"Johnston," she lied and despised her lie as he sensed it for what it was.

"Ten or fifteen minutes."

After no more than two or three minutes she could no longer bear the intense scrutiny, the whispered exchanges, the bursts of bitter laughter, the asides deliberately whispered just loud enough for her to hear

Fenian. Teague. Wee Fenian hoor.

"Lost, are ye?" one lad called out.

The others sniggered.

She stepped back out into the rain.

Finally, what she hoped was a taxi pulled up at the kerb – they'd long since given up their identifying roof signs, too many of their colleagues had been lured into a sectarian murder trap that way.

"Taxi for Johnston?" she asked.

Ellen couldn't make out his muttered response, and got in. She watched, powerless, as two of the youths jumped off the bench and pushed in beside her, a third sliding into the front. They said nothing.

Oh God, had she taken their taxi? What was going on?

"Great Victoria Street, please," she said, her voice trembling, and busied herself checking the change in her purse.

As the driver swerved and sped through unfamiliar streets, she had no idea if they were going towards the city or deeper into Loyalist heartland. There were no familiar landmarks. She stared straight ahead, struggled to control her breathing, slow her pounding heartbeat. Surely they must hear it.

She must not think of young people abducted, tortured, left for dead on waste ground simply because of who they were. Or who their attackers thought they were. Occasionally, paramilitaries apologised for mistakes. Rationally, she was taking a taxi to the station to go home. She had never been more frightened in her life. Finally, after an age of at least twenty minutes, she saw familiar buildings and thanked God for her deliverance. It must have been her imagination. These lads were just blagging a free lift into town, and that was all right, wasn't it?

The driver suddenly pulled in at a street corner.

"Two pound fifty. That's as far as I go"

Maybe neither taxed nor insured – or licensed, even. Avoiding the security patrols. She didn't care. Ellen thrust a fiver into his hand and got out. The two youths in the back banged on the window and gestured to her as she turned to find the passenger from the front standing inches from her, leaning in. Cold steel scraped against her neck.

"You're lucky. Don't come our way again, you wee Fenian bitch, whatever you were at. GO!" He screamed at her, jumping back into the front seat as the taxi did a U turn and roared off.

Clutching her bag, Ellen collapsed onto the pavement and vomited into the gutter before stumbling to the station.

At home, washing in the bathroom, she noticed the tiniest red pinprick on her neck, She imagined stopping in a dark cul-de-sac, the knife slitting her throat. And she vomited again until only spasms of bile remained.

It would be years before she told anyone what had happened. What was the point? She'd thought. She had survived.

In a class she had taken many years later, the tutor had explained that trauma takes anything from three to eighteen generations to pass through a society. The accepted figure is nine.

Nine, Ellen had shuddered inwardly. Nine generations, three hundred years. The tutor had added that they, the affected generation, must work for healing, for the first steps towards closure, otherwise the unresolved trauma would surface again and again.

Shortly after that, she'd started counselling.

And back then, Ellen reflects as she steps off the train and begins the short walk to her home, she had in fact been so fortunate. One of the lucky ones. Eimear, the joy of her world, is living and loving life. Robbie is a good young fella; she likes him. Tomorrow, she expects Eimear will be on the phone, bubbling with excitement, to tell her their offer has been accepted,. Ellen will be genuine in her good wishes and ask what they would most like for a new home present, or would money be better? Perhaps Eimear would like to pick out a few pictures or bits and pieces from home to take with her, even to start them off? Maybe best not to ask. Eimear might feel obliged. They will want everything to be a perfect reflection of their own taste, not hers. They dislike sentiment for sentiment's sake. Only survivors share this irrational need to hang on to reminders of the past.

She loves knowing that Eimear will ring her first with the good news. She always does. Ellen is proud of their closeness; that they can talk about anything.

Well, almost anything. There is no need for Eimear to know that for Ellen and many like her, how cruelly disfigured is the geography of the North, every townland synonymous with a bombing or shooting, every place of worship with a funeral, every street with firebombs and stop and searches. That ghosts still walk everywhere, unquiet graves called for justice. That fate will have her discreetly checking murals, flags, kerbstones forever.

The Eimear of legend, when confronting her husband's affair, won him back, then drank a magic potion to ensure they all forgot it. Obliterated it from collective memory. Happy ever after.

If only.

For her, there is no magic potion. No escape from the toxic undercurrent of lived history.

Too much introspection. What Ellen needs, she chides herself, is a good sleep, devoid of dreams.

On the way to work tomorrow, she will stop at the convenience store and buy a New Home card, and watch all morning for the text or a phone call that will celebrate another milestone for her own Peace Child and her love.

What comfort there is, what serenity in knowing they will never feel the need to read the kerbstones.

Joint Enterprise

Three squad cars speed through the tranquil morning in the well-groomed housing development, turning the head of the handful of dog walkers and busy mothers with meandering toddlers who are about at this hour Most are on their way to and from Callaghan's, the sole convenience store within easy walking distance. Among them is Carmel, clutching her canvas shopper which contains, today, a fresh crusty load for lunch, an *Irish News* and her impulse buy and guilty pleasure, a small bar of Turkish Delight. Her steps quicken as she sees the squad cars pull up and stop in a sequence near her house. The police officers, moving as one, empty out of the cars, stride forwards and she sees with horror that they are knocking, hard, on her door. Bad news. It must be bad news. Ellen? Laura? She opens her mouth to call *wait, I'm coming,* but no sound emerges. She tries to run, her legs water underneath her.

Carmel watches, transfixed, as Owen opens the door and a stream of officers disappear behind it before the door closes forever on forty years of small-town life as she knows it.

Now on another balmy late spring morning, Carmel stretches her legs and wiggles her toes, a precursor to opening her eyes for good, savouring the last moments of cocooning warmth under the duvet before facing the day. Beside her, the radio, its volume turned down, murmurs its cyclic news of election campaigning, disasters both natural and constructed. It washes over her, registering at some level a strange reassurance found in the repetition. She drinks down the dregs of the now lukewarm tea that Declan had left for her, rolls over on to her side, and slowly sits up to face the day. Social media tells her that retirement should be *her-time*, to pursue long-held ambitions, socialise with friends, travel, dip into her savings, indulge. Except she can't.

Downstairs, she switches on the kettle automatically. Declan's cereal bowl is rinsed and draining on the rack, as it has been every morning of married life. An early riser, out for his first constitutional of the day, then gone about his business. Lunchtime is 12.30. There is security in ritual, in routine.

Tea brewing, she goes back upstairs to dress, pausing outside Owen's room to listen. Any sound and she'll take him up a cup. Silence. Maybe she'll leave one beside his bed. But she knows how he values his privacy Best leave it.

There is no need to listen at the girls' bedroom door; hasn't been for so many years now. Laura and Ellen, long gone. Carmel knows the room is immaculate, both beds made up, fresh towels, dusted and polished, just in case. Rooms that have rarely been slept in for more than a couple of nights since college and backpacking had come calling.

That's the natural order of things. Isn't it? She hears of people moaning about their grown-up children coming back home, maybe with a grandchild or two in two and weighted with emotional baggage. Complaining about the fractious clash of lifestyles, of having to put their own life on hold.

Carmel can think of nothing better than to see Ellen and Laura walk in the door. Even for a brief visit. Owen is far from the natural order of things. Owen, sleeping his drugged sleep to postpone reality.

Carmel pulls on a pair of discarded black leggings and a voluminous sweatshirt. There's another day's wear in them. Her uniform. No thought required. Everyone dresses casually since lockdown, and who's looking at her, anyway? Sipping her tea, she checked her phone for messages, missed calls. Nothing. The handful of women she had considered good friends have been permanently unavailable since the day the police came calling.

Apart from the cautious platitudes and distanced nods and smiles in the street. Trouble is infectious.

Carmel will keep herself busy around the house until Owen gets up. She checks in the fridge. Plenty of eggs, bacon, a plastic box of leftover soup. Two-thirds of a loaf in the bread bin. That's lunch, sorted. She'll maybe go to Callaghans, later, just to get out of the house. Break the day. Owen might come with her. She knows he won't.

She switches on the television. More rolling news. Channel-hops, to see if anything among the sofa shows and daytime soaps might hold her attention.

In the bathroom, she wipes down surfaces, checks the laundry basket. No need to put on a wash.

Twenty past eleven. On the landing, she listens again, but no sound.

Early yet. It's the tablets, but the doctor thinks it best to keep Owen prescribed. He said Owen could consider weaning him off when he felt stronger. Sleeping tablets, anti-depressants, tranquillizers seem to be mandatory in prison. The whey-faced young men with dead eyes hunched over the ranged tables at visiting times haunt Carmel.. Prisoners of pharmaceutical subjugation, unresponsive to their anguished mothers struggling to make inane small talk. *Are you sleeping well? What's the food like? Can I bring you anything next time?*

Breaking his favourite biscuits into pieces as they were categorised as a security risk if left whole. How? Buying three waterproof jackets before one finally met the exact specifications – had whoever wrote those lists tried shopping for a plain dark jacket with no logos or trim? The petty degradations, the needless humiliation. The prison warders had aborted one visit after Declan took the lid off his styrofoam cup of tea to let it cool. Alarms going off, ongoing alert, evacuation procedures over a simple cup of tea. Hot liquids can be offensive weapons.

Carmel had often wanted to ask for a chemical cushion for

herself. She feels the familiar irritation rising. Owen really should be up by now.

But what is there for him to get up for?

She quickly quashes that line of thought and goes outside to tend the window boxes. There might be someone passing by for a quick chat. She has to keep busy, to fill the day. Stop her thinking so much.

Declan arrives on the dot of half-past to twelve, just as the soup reaches simmering point. She divides it between the two bowls she has set on the corner of the table – a wedding present.

He lifts a slice of bread, begins buttering it, raises his eyes upwards enquiringly.

"Owen?"

"Still sound out. I checked, a couple of times. In case he fancied a cuppa."

He nods.

They eat methodically, in silence. Is she hungry? She doesn't know. She never eats breakfast, now. Doesn't miss it. You'd think she'd lose a few pounds.

She clears plates and bowls, pours the tea, proffers the packet of Rich Tea. Declan takes two.

"I wish he'd try getting up a bit earlier. He might sleep better at night."

The resignation in his tone is what hurts most. The defeat.

It's been almost a year. Eleven months, two weeks and five days. Carmel counts them as surely as she had counted down the days in prison.

"What are you at this afternoon?"

Declan looks up.

"Are you wanting to go out? I can stay."

"Not, not at all. You go on."

"Jamesie is working on an oul engine out the back. I said might take a walk up to help him."

"You do that, sure. Tell him I was asking for him – and Martha."

Already he is shrugging on his jacket, eager to escape the oppressive atmosphere.

He knows nothing about mechanics. Jamesie isn't a close friend. Jamesie and Martha haven't frozen them out, that's all. Declan must find anything preferable to facing the inane routine their marriage has become. This is a house devoid of meaningful communication. Of things that would have been better left unsaid but had created an insurmountable barrier behind which each retreated into their private self-pity.

Declan had walked out of the courtroom when the clerk read out the catalogue of offences in excruciating, explicit detail. She understood why he'd walked, but she could never forgive Declan for leaving her to hear this alone.

"If it had been you, in the dock, you would have been out this door for good," she had told him when they returned to the silent house. "No two ways about it. Gone."

Deep hurt registered in his eyes. He said nothing.

Declan could never forgive her for that. But it was true. They have a new language now.

Carmel is absently watching a couple about their own age searching for a new life in the sun when she hears the floorboards creaking overhead. The toilet flushing. Quietly, she gets up, switches on the kettle as Owen comes in.

"I was just brewing up. Would you like tea?"

Casual as she can. A quick appraisal. Owen's dressed. A good sign.

"Thanks, Mammy."

"Anything to eat? Will I put you on some toast?"

"I'm not hungry yet. Thanks."

They take their cups and sit down in adjoining armchairs.

"What are you watching?"

"Ach, it's just one of those silly house-hunting programmes. I wasn't following it. Turn it over if you like."

"It's grand."

He stares straight at the screen, sipping his tea.

What's going on in his head?

It is Carmel's pain that she has never really known. Her baby, such an easy child, unlike his elder sisters who could be wilful, feisty. His primary school teachers said that while he struggled to keep up, there was never a day's bother with him. *Pleasan*t and *well-behaved* were words that dominated his reports.

How was school today? She'd ask. Owen would smile at her, that beautiful, gentle smile, and say nothing. He'd play happily on his own, in his room. Carmel was always weary from working part-time and running the home and it had been a blessing not to worry about what he was up to. Secondary school followed, the pattern set.

Everything all right, son?

The same smile.

No running the roads, no hanging round the street corners, no bother with girls – or boys, she had considered that possibility, too, though they say a mother always knows. A few friends who'd call round in the evenings, after he starting working in the warehouse. They'd go up to his room, maybe have a few cans, play on his X box or whatever they called it, chat away on the Internet.

Carmel had congratulated herself on how safe he was. Never any bother with Owen.

Until the day the police arrived at the door,

The kindly young policewoman had taken her aside and explained that Owen had made verbal statements. He was going willingly, that there was nothing to be alarmed about. She, Carmel, couldn't have known. Not to blame herself. Then she'd made her a cup of her own tea as Carmel struggled for any shred of comprehension.

Owen made a full admission. He hadn't even waited for a solicitor. Not an ounce of guile in him. She and Declan had sorted that, later. The solicitor, a matter-of-fact, weary man with professional expertise in cases like Owen's, explained patiently how these things worked. She had shuddered at words like *international paedophile pornography ring*s; could not equate them with her Owen. *Clickbait.*

How opening a tiny image could somehow lure you into a word of degradation and exploitation, seduce you into downloading, which was categorised as making an image even if you wouldn't know how; sharing and liking. The solicitor had guided Declan and her through the unfamiliar world of category three and category four offences and what they implied, through the protracted waiting outside courtrooms for remands, referrals, until finally it was almost a relief when the day of sentencing came. Carmel heard the judge describe this person in the dock, pale and shaking in his new grey suit, as to be given credit for his early and full admission and plea, but *the gravity of this kind of offence could not be overlooked....*

That was her baby. Her Owen.

Five years.

He had served half of that in prison, far from home. In isolation, for his own safety. He would be serving the real sentence for the rest of his life.

So would they.

Golden beaches, azure blue seas and skies, dazzling white apartment blocks and tavernas bustling with cheerful people shine from a television screen that neither of them is watching.

*Talk to me, Owen. Tell me why. Tell me what it was like in prison. Tell me what I can do no*w.

"Do you fancy another cuppa?" Carmel hears her anodyne question and despises herself. This has to stop.

"I'm grand, thank, Mammy."

"Owen, you're not grand. You're a twenty-eight-year-old man who spends his days lying in bed or watching daytime television, doing nothing, seeing no-one. That's far from grand. When did you last go for a walk? When did you last speak to anybody other than me and your Da?"

Carmel cannot believe she has just said this. She looks for the hurt in his eyes but sees only indifference.

"Owen."

"I'm sorry, Ma. I've told you – I'm sorry."

Owen had signed the Register, indefinitely. Carmel hadn't realised the gravity of its implications. About contact with children, even family, and vulnerable adults, which seemed to her to be a very wide-ranging category. No Smartphone, no Internet. How could he hope to find work?

Carmel struggles to keep the conversation going over the tea table. No, they hadn't got far with the engine. They'd gone to meet Martha off the bus and she'd insisted on making them all cappuccinos with her fancy new machine that you just have to slide wee capsules into and it comes out all frothy, though Jamesie says the wee capsules are a terrible price altogether. But then a cappuccino in the Country Kitchen is £3.40 now. It's all far from what they were reared on and, apart from three days in Rome on a pilgrimage before her wedding in 1976, Martha has never set foot in Italy and never will again.

Why are we talking like this? This isn't our language, Carmel thinks, *It's trivia, it's a parody of small-town life fabricated to fill the void between us. We would have laughed at us, once.*

The table cleared, Owen does the dishes, methodically. They watch the news, national and local. Declan interjects only occasionally to bemoan the state of society. Then, as the soaps began, he gets to his feet.

"I think I'll just head out for a couple of pints. See who's about."

"Right. Enjoy yourself."

"I'll be back before ten."

"No worries."

She knows he will sit in a dark corner, taciturn and uncommunicative, nursing his pint, absorbed in introspection.

She glances at Owen.

"Would you fancy going with your Da? Even for a wee while?"

Again, the response is instant. Owen shakes his head.

"Thanks, though."

Carmel feels foolish for suggesting it when they all know the answer. More role-playing in a scenario none of them devised.

Declan edges towards the door. Guilty in his escape.

She flicks through a couple of magazines so old she could recite their contents.

"I was thinking I should order some wool. Get started on a wee cardigan or two for New Zealand."

Her elder daughter, Laura, settled in Auckland with the plush house and the big handsome husband they have never met, expecting their first grandchild in September. *What need would she have for an Aran pram set, far from home? Will she ever get to cuddle this child?* New Zealand is so far away; no word of Laura ever coming back for a visit. She will be a distanced Granny, a weekly Face-time call away.

"Owen, would you like a coffee? Or a hot chocolate? I fancy a drink, myself."

He comes into the kitchen as she is pouring.

"Chocolate, please. That's great, Mammy. I'll take it upstairs."

Already?

"Are you tired, son?"

"There's not much on the telly. Think I'll play my Xbox for a bit."

"You Da'll be home in an hour if you want to come down and have a bite of supper with us?"

"Maybe. I'll see."

That means no.

A last bid.

"If it's nice in the morning, I fancy a bit of a walk. I never got out of the house at all today."

He just smiles. She knows he won't go. Nor will she. They haven't been out as a family since the arrest. Even to Mass. She who had castigated her daughters for not attending.

Sitting in the kitchen, her library book open but unread, she hears the aggressive sound effects from whatever he's playing. At least he hasn't gone to bed yet. At ten o'clock, as precise as his father, he will take the sleeping tablet that seems to give him twelve hours or more of oblivion.

It isn't right, she can't pretend it's right. Not even to herself, but then nothing is right any more. She fetches her box of Merlot from the press and pours herself a generous glass. She likes to buy the boxes, now, as they last from one week to the next and besides, they're more economic, glass for glass. No bottles to recycle. Soon, Carmel knows she will feel calmer. Alcohol is a sedative, not unlike her son's medication.

The weeks roll by, slowly but securely. Shopping on a Friday. The Face-time call to New Zealand early on a Sunday morning, to allow for the time difference. And, she suspects, so that Laura and her big successful, handsome husband will conveniently miss Owen, who is inevitably in bed. Ellen likes to message. Voice notes, she calls them. Ellen wants her to come over for a visit. Says she'd treat Carmel to a spa experience, a shopping spree. She'll even get the plane tickets. But would Dermot and Owen cope in their binary orbit? Carmel would be stressing about it the minute she got on the airport bus.

Sitting in the silence, Carmel suddenly remembers a drama she'd watched on television, years ago. It was about a young lad who got caught up in a revenge attack that ended with a man dead. He'd only been in the car, getting a lift, or something – she couldn't quite remember. He hadn't known what the others were going to do. Still, they were all charged with the same offence. Murder. Joint Enterprise was the legal term for it. She'd got drawn into the drama, felt sorry for the lad, for his mother. The poor woman might as well have been in the dock herself. She stuck by him.

Joint Enterprise.

That's it, she realises. That's what I've been convicted of. Joint Enterprise. I was downstairs in the house while all this was going on. I didn't know. But that young lad didn't know, either. Nor his mother. And we have all been found guilty. We are all serving a life sentence. Within our own four walls. A life sentence nonetheless.

Enough, Carmel.

She drains the glass, pours more wine, just a top up, and drinks it down quickly.

Enough. This cannot go on. And only I can stop it.

Before she has time to think, she grabs the wine box and empties it down the sink, her finger pressed firmly on the pour button till it is empty. She lifts her phone. Ellen knows full well how difficult it would be for her to get away, so she will invite Ellen here. Book them an overnight spa break nearby, everywhere does them now, if that's what Ellen wants. The men can manage for one night. If Ellen doesn't want to face the facts about her brother, let her say so. No more hypocrisy, no more hiding. She will text Laura, suggest an alternative time for the Sunday call, one when she knows Owen will be there, even if he says nothing. She will send a group text to her three oldest friends, cheerfully apologising for being *off the radar* and proposing to meet for lunch in two weeks' time. At least then she will know who has cut all ties and who was too awkward to get in touch. She will go online and get the syllabus for classes at the Women's Centre – *slow down Carmel, Baby steps.*

It is a cruel irony that the support services count Owen as one of their successes. Safe in the care of a loving and supportive family, all post-sentence programmes completed, Owen has escaped the revolving door cycle of offending that already has most of his fellow inmates back in prison. Owen is effectively off their books now. It is up to her, but also, she now realises, up to him too. And up to Declan, how he chooses to live his life.

Declan.

She glances up at the kitchen clock. Nearly ten. Time to boil the kettle for Declan's supper.

The Magic Roundabout

Lil wakes to *The Need*. *The Need* precedes *The Fear*. *The Need* jerks her out of deep, unnatural sleep. It's 4am. She doesn't need to lift her alarm clock to her face to know. 4am. The Need strikes when the body is at its lowest. *The Need* for the all-enveloping relief when the panacea of that first shot burns down the throat, glows the gut and cauterises every frazzled nerve ending. The total relaxation into that warm numbness that can't last, and is only mocked by every shot that follows as inexorably as she knows it will, until oblivion subsumes everything. Because from the moment you swallow, she knows, you are back on that magic roundabout, round and round as it spins faster and faster and the only way off it is to plunge into the hell that awaits.

But that will not be today. Today is not a day to face *The Fear*. Maybe tomorrow. Or the day after.

So here she is, four o'clock on a spring morning – Saturday, she registers, thank God it's a Saturday, trapped in the labyrinthine mental trail between closing time and the early supermarket opening. Lil needs a drink. Her fingers trail the floor beside the bed. Nothing. Where, for Christ's sake, can she have put the bottle? What sort of insane motive compels her to hide it in a house where she lives alone?

She leans across to pull open the bedside drawer, fingers probing among the moisturisers and pill packets. Nothing. She flicks on the light. A scrawl on the notepad, then, below it, an attempt to print legibly.

Window sill.

She rolls out, crawls across to the window.

Don't question, just check how much there is left. Pease let it be a half, nearly a half. It won't be but, please, please, a quarter full.

Relief floods her, her heart rate slows. Around a third, maybe even just under half. Half of a half, her second of the night. Or her third? Think, girl, think.

But enough. Enough, perhaps, to put her over again, to see her through until the supermarket opens at eight. Then the shakes mollified, she will swipe her credit card for a replacement, walk fast to the toilets, twist off the cap and two good gulps to see her round to the taxi rank and home.

Sinking into the pillow, Lil savours the warmth, the sense of the duvet hugging her, swaddling, secure. No need to sleep just yet. Time to tease out the moment, to tell herself her own bedtime story, her dream of a happy ending.

Lil wakes again, just after seven, suddenly alert. She rubs the caked gunge from her eyes, scraping it out of the corners. Mouth dry, head pounding, legs twitching involuntarily. Spasms. She rolls out of bed and, clutching the bottle, walks slowly and unsteadily to the kitchen. Pours water. Tries to sip it. Gulps it instead. Retches. It takes four attempts before the bitter bile is unstoppable and she makes it through to the bathroom, clutching the cold porcelain, bringing up what little is in her stomach.

When did she last eat?

Thursday?

What trickles from her mouth is clear, acidic. Every retch hurts but is also a relief. She sticks her fingers down her throat, trying to bring up more. Spoonfuls at a time. Soon, she is exhausted. She pulls herself up to sit on the toilet and pee. The trickle is burning and reeks of acetone. Her bowel spasms, but there's nothing there. Stale sweat trickles down her face with every movement. Lodges in every crevice of her body. She wants to take a bath. But not yet.

Lil makes it back to the kitchen, a step at a time, clutching the door jamb, the worktops. She pours more water and rinses out her mouth.

She glances in the makeup mirror. Eyes red-rimmed and streaked with pink veins. Flushed cheeks, the first sign of broken capillaries. Lil runs a comb through matted hair, clips it up and applies a thin layer of makeup. She is fooling no one. She is hoping not to attract comment in the supermarket. A random application of body spray. Thank God she had the discipline to charge the phone. She scavenges a few pound coins and a fiver from a savings jar. For emergencies. Taxi money. This is an emergency. Seven forty-five. She rings the taxi. Five minutes.

Carefully, so carefully, she lifts the bottle. Pours what's left into a mug. One drink, two. She puts on her sunglasses, picks up her bag, and carries the mug to the door. She'll only finish it when the taxi arrives.

Seven fifty-five and Lil is in the back of the taxi speeding the quick journey to the supermarket, which will just be opening. Already, her hands are steadier, her stomach settling. She presses the five-pound note on the driver and says a polite thank you without making eye contact She is always polite. She drops the coins on the pavement and fumbles for them before walking, almost running into the supermarket.

Straight to the off licence section. A bottle of own brand gin; something to get her rehydrated. Cider? A litre, budget brand; she has never liked the taste. Have they 8.6 lager? Probably not. Or Lambrini, sickly sweet but easily downed? No, the cider is better. The array of bright labels and clever packaging dazzles her, so pretty, so inviting. On some impulse, she lifts two cans of ready-mixed cocktails that scream 'party'. Checkout. It's just opening. So slow. She swipes her card, asks for some cash back, bags it in her opaque carried and hurries to the toilets, not caring who notices.

Lil grasps a can. The ring pulls breaks. Sweating again, she manages to open the other and gulps from it, dribbling the sticky chemical sweetness over her chin. Lil crushes it and slides it down the metal chute into the sanitary bin beside the bowl. She twists the cap off the gin – carefully, in case it cracks and she has to hold it upright all the way home in the taxi. One drink. Two. Three. She is coming alive. She flushes the toilet, goes out the back and gets into a taxi.

Going home is slower as she has hit peak time traffic, people going about their business. Frustrated, she leans forward in the seat and, head low, tries to raise the bottle to her mouth.

Lil runs in the door and collapses on the floor behind it, but nothing can touch her now. She has her supplies, her oblivion. Upstairs to the bedroom, shut the door, switch on the radio for company. She realises how sore her back is. Her lower back. Kidneys? And it's so hot. She opens the window, relief from the chilly breeze, normality from the traffic passing by. She decides she'd better drink some cider, as she's so thirsty. Lil stashes the gin in the bedside drawer. The morning magazine programme engages her, promises of fun weekends ahead, days out, good company.

Sometime around nine, she slides open the drawer, takes out the gin and drinks. She wants more sleep. She wants oblivion.

Coming round, Lil checks the clock. After three. That's good. Time to sort the rest of the day. Time to buy more. Just in case. Mustn't repeat last night. More cider, a quick gin and slowly downstairs, clutching the bannister. She's too tired to go out again. Everything is an effort. But, she must act quickly to dispel the anxiety. The Fear. She rings the off licence with the delivery service; they take a half hour or more. Orders another bottle of gin. Wishes she had ice. Wishes she had lime cordial. Supermarket? Too much. Lil switches on the television for company. She wishes she was at the state where she could get out of the house, to browse the shops, to go into a pub and have a drink in a corner. She's a bit hungry; could pick up a filled sub roll – that'd be good. Two. But it's too risky. What if she falls? Or passes out? No way is she doing another detox in hospital, tubed up and not enough morphine to get her through, counting the hours till the next two tranquillisers. She'll start it here. Tomorrow.

The delivery arrives. Lil drinks from a glass in front of the telly. She takes down favourite books, a pad and pen. Her hands are steady. She is happy now. She writes, scribbles ideas, plans. Lil wants to talk to someone. An old friend? Someone she loves? Loved? She just wants to talk, not to be alone. Maybe she should ring just to let someone know she's OK.

 But she was at work yesterday. Functioning. Why would she not be OK?

Maybe she shouldn't.

When she wakes again, it is dark.

After seven. That's seven in the evening. This second bottle of gin is about a third gone. How did that happen? How much is left in the bottle beside the bed? Lil needs a bottle to get through the night. Should she order another? Her stomach cramps, needs sustenance. There is nothing in the house that she fancies. Beans? There are definitely tins of beans in the cupboard. She never seems to eat them. There's no bread for toast. Lil lifts a menu from the television shelf and orders for delivery. Another twenty minute wait.

A glass of gin poured, and she is all go again. With an unsustainable burst of energy, Lil tidies the room, makes a coffee that she will not drink, and a hot water bottle for her aching back, gets a plate and fork, consults the TV guide. The food arrives, hot and greasy, soaking through the paper. She needs the cider. Crawls upstairs, checks the gin while she's there. Just over a half. Lil does the sums. She's slightly worried. She needs to factor in her morning drink. The supermarket doesn't open till one on a Sunday and the convenience store doesn't sell alcohol till eleven, or is it half past? Should she get a third bottle? How? Could she order another delivery? Would they notice? Would they care?

It will be half an hour. More. It'll be busier now. Lil leaves the door open and watches out the window, ready to grab it from the driver when he arrives. She struggles not to drink any more until then. The food gets tepid, the fat congealing into cloudy windows on the wrapper. She can always microwave it.

Relief floods through Lil as she grabs the bottle and shuts the door in the man's face. Is it the same driver? Who knows?

A woman she'd got to know in group therapy – dead now, she supposes – had told her of the magic roundabout in a city where she had once lived and drunk. A woman much sicker than she – *stop! Comparisons are invidious and can she now say this with conviction?*

The woman – Ann, Annie? – had chuckled wryly as she described how, in the slow, desperate hours after the late clubs and pubs shut and the early shops opened, a young girl she had palled up with one random night had led her, stumbling on party heels, to a roundabout near an off-licence that was known for selling cut price booze to anyone who had the means to pay, regardless of what state they were in. A street drinkers' offie. She had watched as her companion pulled off her stiletto and dug deep into the soil around the municipal marigolds until her hand closed on the neck of a half-bottle recently buried in a shallow grave. She pulled it out, triumphant. This was where the alkies kept their cure, their emergency stash, she said; they couldn't take drink into the night shelters. Safe till the morning, she grinned. Fuck that. Cheers! She'd raised a toast and made a two-fingered sign at the hostel across the street where the owner presumably slept unaware. She pressed back the soil, smoothed it over. You'd find more if you dug deeper, she added, confident in her authority now, but she wasn't into stuff like that, never had been, drugs were for mugs. But it had never let her down, she claimed. The Magic Roundabout. God Bless it.

There is nothing magic about her roundabout today. What Lil knows in her core is that she is gripping tight to it, spinning faster and faster, out of control, occasionally exhilarated, sometimes giddy, powerless to stop its centrifugal force, terrified of the moment when letting go and crashing to earth can no longer be put off. When her body cannot physically endure one more spin. Even if she kids herself, she can for one fleeting, euphoric moment. It is not a roundabout. It is upended, it is her treadmill. Round and round, painful and punishing, and no way to get off for good.

Lil puts the bottle in the cupboard behind the beans, writes a note to herself where it is, hopes she amends the note if she decided takes a notion to move it in the night. Can't face a frantic search. Maybe she'll have that bath now. Freshen up. A bedtime ritual. They're supposed to be relaxing. Therapeutic.

Another burst of energy. Food into the fridge. Two slow trips upstairs with the glass, the gin, the cider. Phone and charger. Notepad and pen. The room is lovely and cool. Outside, it is raining. She switches on the radio to have company later and makes a gin and cider cocktail for the bath.

Lil has her happiest hour before sleep, her mind replaying good times from the past, dreaming of the future. What she'd do if she won the Lotto. What she'd do if she could revisit the lost child inside her, make it better for her.

What she wishes she'd done for the other lost child – *stop. Stop. Not now.* Lil needs peace to sleep.

Clumsily, she decants the leftover gin into one bottle. Splashes soak into the carpet.

Half full. Half empty. Will she be able to get downstairs in the night if she needs to? She dozes and wakes to the shipping forecast. Her eyes burn, back aches. She is sweating and shivering at once.

North Utsire, South Utsire, Forties

She imagines huge breakers, rugged rock scapes, brooding storm clouds

Cromarty, Forth, Tyne, Dogger

Sweeping down through Scotland, England. Where we drove on childhood holidays, the cramped confinement in the back seat, the nausea, the stop off at the Little Chef for golden flat pancakes that were nothing like our home-made pancakes, with wee sachets of maple syrup.

Portland, Plymouth, Biscay, Trafalgar

Naval battles, seafaring adventure. She loved history class at school. She liked the girls she sat beside. They did projects together. A reconstructed Navan Fort, an appliqué English Queen.

Irish Sea, Shannon, Rockall, Malin

The night before her baby was born, she couldn't sleep. She lay uncomfortably in the stiff bed in the maternity unit, listening to the same forecast… connecting to the wider world. It is still out there and she is no longer a part of it.

Her baby. No longer a baby. She misses her baby. Panic surges.

Stop, stop,

You made your choice.

Except it wasn't a choice.

Irish Sea, Shannon, Rockall, Malin

The impotent lullaby of the sleepless

"*Wake up, mammy, wake up.*"

Weeping, tiny arms around her, anxious white face staring into hers as she struggled to open her eyes, slumped on the stairs where a friend would find her.

Does he miss me?

Does anyone miss me?

She misses her baby.

I have stolen his life

I have stolen mine

Hot tears of self-pity.

More drinking. More craving oblivion.

How much does it take now?

She knows the answer.

Into the third bottle by morning.

I want to sleep

I don't want to wake up

I want this to be over.

I can't live with drink. I can't live without it.

* * * *

It is not the next day but the one after when Lil wakes up and knows it is enough. Monday. A three-day bender. The usual. A tremulous call to work.

A virus, they agree. Yes, she's ringing the doctor. Off for three or four days.

Does anyone believe it? Does anyone care?

She lies for as long as she can before crawling downstairs. She rations that last bottle. A unit an hour. Then a unit every two hours. Shakes, sweats. The pain in her back is excruciating, whether she walks, sits, stands or lies. Her stomach is raw. She imagines a slab of pulsating liver, dark and bloody. Her head pounds, her eyes burn deep in their sockets. Dehydration. She can't keep down water. Her system is geared to cope with alcohol, craving the poison.

She rings the doctor, holding on through a tinny cyclic destruction of Sibelius. There are no appointments. She wouldn't be able to get to one. She goes on a list of house calls – the receptionist senses the urgency – and leaves the door ajar while she lies on the sofa in this hell of her own making.

Why?

Find your why, a counsellor had once advised.

Then you can find your why not.

Simplistic bitch. Well meaning, but simplistic. If it was that easy...

For they are just sections of the same roundabout, forever revolving,

Drink has destroyed life. Sometimes – less often now, she justifies to herself. It has been – not since Christmas, so what, three months? But it happens. She cannot cope with what she has done. It takes over, and she is on the roundabout again, spinning and shrieking with a terrible and terrified animation, before she jumps and falls, as she knows she must.

Why?

She sits by the toilet bowl, the cool ceramic and the retching strangely comforting. The feeling of emptiness, of ritual cleansing.

She presses her cheek hard against the tiled floor, inhaling the acrid smell of bleach and disinfectant. It is comforting.

A doctor comes. Dispenses the familiar white tablets. Tears of gratitude. Of relief. They will help a little, she knows. Always means to save a couple for emergencies. Always needs the lot. Lil is to call into the surgery tomorrow for more. Clearly, she is a risk – no week's supply for her.

She battles through the sleepless night.

Cromarty, Forth, Tyne, Dogger.

She wants to down what's left in that last bottle, so much. And then buy just one more. She fantasises about ordering in.

Why? Why not?

Irish Sea, Shannon, Rockall, Malin

The impotent lullaby of the sleepless

The next day she bathes, washes her hair, puts on fresh clothes and takes a taxi to the health centre for her tablets. She's not well enough to walk that far. She crosses the street to the convenience store and buys Lucozade, painkillers, doorstop sandwiches. Boiled sweets to make her mouth taste better. Milkshakes for her furrowed gut. Cash from the machine.

By the second day after the second sleepless night, she is writing to-do lists. Somehow she finds he strength to change the sweat-sodden sheets, put on a wash, open windows and blow the sweet stale gin smell from the house. Walks to the health centre and shop, though she needs a taxi back, exhausted.

By the third day, Lil is drinking coffee and feeling hungry. The pain is subsiding. The shakes have gone. Her bin filled, the house tidy. She can walk easily. Considers going up the town to fill the day. Treat herself to a cappuccino. That night, the third, sleep comes as she knows it will. For five blessed hours.

She is ready to take tentative steps back to the world. She rings work, says she will be in to see them on Friday, back on Monday.

But *The Fear* paralyses her. It is back, living in her head, a constant taunt.

You are a waste
A failure
You can never undo the damage, make reparation for the hurt and destruction you have caused
No one wants you
You despise yourself
Why fight it? Why go on?

Lil functions through the blackness, as she must.

She knows she is suicidal. Sober and suicidal.

A colleague gets in touch to see if she's feeling better.

She must know? Does it matter?

Soon, she says....We will meet up soon. Coffee. Look forward to it.

It'll fill an afternoon, one weekend.

The darkness closes in as she hugs her coffee.

She misses her baby.

Her baby that is no longer a baby, or even a child.

And whose fault is it?

Exactly.

I don't deserve her.

Get on with it, Lil hears her mother's voice echo down the years. *Just get on with it. Make the best of things; that's what we all had to do.*

She will be back to the mundane, the routine. Filling her days with the same timetables. Keeping busy. Keeping what they call *well*. Exercise. Self care. Work. She has no more tablets. No more oblivion.

Until the next time.

Maybe there won't be a next time.

Wouldn't it be perfect to think so?

Even she doesn't believe that, any more than the doctor. Or her counsellor.

Or the young woman, so lost to her now, who was once her baby.

Matchstick Man

It was that daft woman with the scarves who seemed to have some direct inroads into the council coffers that had started it all. Until then, Ronnie recalled, they'd been quite happy to pot a few balls round the dilapidated pool table, watch the horse racing or the game shows on the telly in the corner, leaf through coffee-stained copies of last week's local papers. Some of the old boys played dominoes. Banter, directed at no one in particular. Endless boiling of kettles, trays of tea and value brand biscuits. A smoking balcony that was always busy, ashtrays overflowing with roll up butts, inspirational messages tacked to the railing.

"Keep it Simple."

"One Day at a Time."

One Day at a Time, Sweet Jesus, some wit would burst into song, walking past, now and again. It was a tired old joke. As tired as the rest of them. Cashing their Giro, buying their drink at the offie down below – the good stuff on a Thursday, maybe even through the weekend, strong lager and sickly sweet British wine by Monday morning – swallowing a cure, shakes subsiding enough to climb the rickety stairs adjoining the premises to the day centre. Handing over their precious bottle or can to Maggie in the office, waiting while she wrote their name on it in felt pen, locked it in the cupboard, ready for its revolving door trips punctuating the day ahead.

Tea, more tea, endless bloody tea, anything to fill the hours ahead without diluting their sedation too much.

Then She'd come prancing in. Madame Bloody Butterfly.

They'd had advance notice from Martin. Martin, the support worker – he was all right, Martin, as long as he didn't get all intense on you – he was studying for a certificate, you'd see him poring over these tomes on theories of addiction and positive individual recognition. Something to do with a celebration of culture, he recalled Martin explaining. Recognising artistic expressions of identity.

"We are all artists," Martin had read from the council letter and, of course, Dinny had interjected, "Aye, piss artists."

It was a poor joke; all Dinny's jokes were pathetic, but the obligatory laughter had drowned out the core message. After that, he hadn't a clue.

Until She'd come prancing in. Five feet and a cough, age indeterminate, marital status also – Dinny was taking bets, the odds changing as more of them reckoned no one could stick her – all these silky, bright coloured scarves draped around her diminutive frame. Circling her neck, shrouding her head, tying back her hair, even holding up her jeans. A riot of colour across her signature black. *Performance black,* she had told them.

Who or what the performance was for, he had no idea.

But Martin had been firm. There was money in it and God knows the centre was always short of money, always under threat of closure. In times of austerity, the public consciousness favoured neonatal units and cancer wards over day care for committed and unrepentant drinkers – or *substance abusers* as they were now known. Or was it *users?* The terms kept diluting to keep pace with social correctness.

So, if they wanted a roof over their head in an overheated day room, their free Primark clothes parcel at Christmas, a midday meal, for those that bothered, and the endless tea, they'd better take part.

Money was no object, it seemed. Canvases and acrylics for the group haphazardly tackling cognitive painting on a Tuesday morning. Digital recorders for the oral historians telling their life story, or an apocryphal version of it, for your woman to transcribe. Winnie, poor sad Winnie, was knitting wee people for a wall hanging representing life in the centre, instead of pink and blue cardigans for the grandchildren she never saw and who must, Ronnie reckoned, be heading for their teens now.

Damo, who hadn't been at himself since he got out after eighteen years, and had more to worry him than the drink, was supposed to be painting pictures and messages on flat polished stones. Made a change from pegging them. So long as he didn't take one of his turns and try to swallow them. Martin kept an eye out. You could rely on Martin.

And Ronnie?

He would have been tempted to take up smoking again, just to sit on the balcony for the better part of the day, observing this creative insanity from a safe distance. But She had followed him out and, he could still hardly credit it, leapt from her seat to cough, rub her eyes and declare that the ashtray had inspired her. Not to empty it, although it was overflowing onto the table, but to task him with building a matchstick replica of the town hall. Martin, in the spirit of everyone having a back story, had disclosed that he'd been a practising architect in a past life. A life that seemed to have happened to someone else. Fuck Martin anyway. But he meant well.

The next Tuesday, when She unloaded yet more blank canvases, garish coloured tubes of paint, virgin brushes for the Art Group to smear their inner thoughts with, he was presented with a sketch pad, a box of 2HB pencils, printed images of the town hall, taken from every angle, including an aerial shot of the roof. And a massive box of matchsticks. Glue would be handed over when he was ready and kept under lock and key as securely as the tonic wine and the 8.6 lager. Not that he'd ever indulged. He was of an earlier generation. Very few cross addicts. Or users.

Another pep talk from Martin about their public showcase in June. There was no escape. Ronnie preferred working alone. The drawing of the scale model had been a challenge, but had revived skills he had long forgotten he had. The daytime hours that usually dragged sped by. He took only the number of trips outside required to keep his hands steady. Many evenings, when the centre closed at eight o'clock, he was surprised how much drink he had left to see him through the walk home to his bedsit and the long night ahead.

When the ground floor was in place, he felt stirrings of pride. Even when She clapped her tiny hands and waxed lyrical over it, disappointed only that he hadn't counted the number of matches involved, proclaiming it the showcase's centrepiece, it didn't devalue it. Hardly a compliment. What competition was there? – Dinny must have used fifty quid's worth of paint and canvas recreating the contents of his stomach spewed on the pavement on a good Saturday night – he didn't let his usual self-sabotaging streak stop his progress. Martin was ecstatic. Ronnie could have floated on the number of cups of tea left at his workstation, built a fortress round the construction out of uneaten custard creams.

* * * *

Ronnie had never meant to let his model get beyond the foundations, or perhaps the first floor. Just enough to ensure the centre got the funding it needed, and as a gesture to Martin who was a good soul who could undoubtedly have secured a cosier position at one of the city's many day centres for older adults: same pointless crafting, uneaten dinners, mindless television, same service users, as they were termed, dozing out the monotony of their days, same random, repetitive and fragmented conversations, if you could even call them that, same acrid smells of stale urine, poor personal hygiene and bodies decaying from the inside out. But without the endless loop of having to get up every turnaround to unlock the alcohol, see its owner off the premises, let them in again half an hour or half a day later to repeat. Plus the accompanying verbals. Not to mention the random eruptions of violence.

Not for Her, mind you, with her text book liturgy of positive enrichment, inner voices, latent talent reserves, transferable skills. It wasn't for Her.

Wasn't he only doing a cruel parody of what he'd done for a living until he'd let the drink take it away? He'd been a functioning alcoholic for years, perhaps not as undetected as he'd like to believe. He was a quiet, solitary drinker, not given to outbursts of aggression, of raucous roistering, profanity or maudlin weeping. Then one day, as surely as he had, in truth, known for some years it would, there was one professional disaster that had cost his firm a significant contract and with it their reputation and cost him his job and his future employability. When he'd walked out of the obligatory rehab after two and a half weeks, it had cost him his home and family, too.

As the date of the showcase approached, more than once, he'd felt that familiar self-destructive streak rising within him. *Walk away*, it had whispered, as She'd buzzed round the room, swathed in her latest finery, a fringed effrontery bedecked with a caravan of purple and blue camels plodding beneath a cerise sunset. She had been in raptures at Dinny's canvases: *Such power! Such freedom of expression!* The newly discovered Jackson Pollock of daycare had sat beaming, abashed as an adolescent youth before a favourite teacher. Winnie's unstructured pastel people stapled to the hessian backcloth on which was painted an outline of the room, so randomly proportioned his trained eye told him it was a structural impossibility. Winnie's dropped stitches hung down like ovoid pink and blue teardrops. Damo's stones assembled on a piece of ochre felt, representing the sand of the seashore, their runic messages undecipherable even to the artist himself. He later told Ronnie he'd copied one or two from the tattoos on his brother's neck. When Ronnie asked him what the tattoos meant, he'd stared at him blankly as if it was a ridiculous question. For those who couldn't, wouldn't, or didn't, through disinterest, physical inability or incapacitation, Martin had helped Her to arrange abstract displays of billiard balls held in place with Blu Tack beside crossed cues, and a tumbling ramble of dominoes across a cracked board. Together, they were captioned "Daily Life."

* * * *

With three days to go, Madame Butterfly and Martin had to shoo away the fellow service users who hovered on Ronnie's periphery, watching him put the roofing in place. The clock had been the most exacting. He'd taken it home to measure, cut, glue, and varnish during one of his usual sleepless nights. Ronnie forswore tea, banned the hourly delivery. His trips to the bottle safe were minimal: no big deal; he'd always been able to stop for days, weeks, even a few months at a time. He could feel the air of unlooked-for respect, admiration. The rest of them weren't entirely daft. They knew their artwork was shite; they were just playing the game. There could be a year's heating oil in it, thermal fleeces and new trainers all round.

At a quarter to eight on the eve of the showcase, Ronnie tapped his brush on the edge of the varnish tin, secured the lid and pulled back his chair. He'd always needed a deadline. His town hall stood before them, proud and gleaming. Far from perfect, he knew – what a job he might have made of it once! – but to scale, obsessively neat, a model to merit its place in any exhibition, not merely one for – what were they now? – the severely disadvantaged and marginalised.

Martin took photos on his phone for social media. No faces, of course. There was a round of spontaneous applause. Just a sign to write, though it was self-explanatory. He'd do that at home. As the emerging artists straggled out of the centre to walk to bedsits, hostels, or the streets, Ronnie was the last to leave. He found himself flanked by the Fringed Muse on the left and Martin on the right.

"…absolutely remarkable…surpassed all my expectations…." he tried to block out her effusive twittering, hoped they'd shake her off at the first car park they came to.

He neither desired nor needed this. He'd done what he'd said he would. What more did she want?

Stopping at the Pay Station, she touched his arm.

"Really," she was saying, "really I see enormous opportunities for you here."

Small grants, set-ups, business support, working from home…

his patience tested as he waited for her inevitable conclusion, *and though it's not usual*, I know, *I'm confident I could secure funding for a second spell in rehab....*

He caught Martin flashing her a warning look, but she was oblivious, a woman on a mission. Ronnie smiled politely, gritted his teeth and strode ahead.

Alone in the bedsit, he pulsed with anger. He paced the room. Paced it again. Made tea. Left it to get cold. Made another cup. It got cold, too. It was displacement activity – he didn't want it. Wasn't hungry. Switched on the news – usual rubbish. Switched it off again. He'd left his bottle in the lock-up; so what? He had money in his pocket to buy more, but he knew nothing short of oblivion would quell this rage.

Why? All the suppressed self-loathing, of course, for what he'd had and drunk away. No rosy nostalgia; it had been an average semi, a routine if secure job, an acceptable, childless marriage. A routine. He'd been getting by. But it hadn't been enough. And he hadn't been enough to walk away, start again. Hence the drink. Just as now he was getting by, walking to and from the day centre, minding his business, occasionally helping to defuse fraught situations among the more volatile. And for the past three months, measuring, cutting and glueing thousands of matchsticks to guarantee enough heating oil to ensure a group of hapless, vulnerable individuals didn't freeze to death on the city streets and cause a civic embarrassment. Why not bypass the ridiculous project and give the money squandered on canvases and paints, varnish and glue and matchsticks straight to Martin? What sort of fantastical artistic vision had he allowed himself to be caught up in? He was guilty of collusion in this exercise in civic obfuscation. Dinny was right, that first week – why not give them the money to go on one massive two day piss up away from the city and let the council take round the visiting dignitaries in their absence? No danger of civic embarrassment, then. No risk of a PR tour coming upon a broken body prone on a pavement, of shattered glass and vomit defacing an arts installation.

Her mentioning fresh starts, though. Rehab. That was what had done it. He was not a violent man, never had been, but the urge to tell her where to go, her and take with her, her arts strategies and her social analysis that bore no relation to his life had overwhelmed him. She hadn't lived, for God's sake. They had.

He pulled on his jacket and strode out again, jingling the coins in his pocket, fingering the notes. He felt better, already. The warm glow of contentment was soothing the frayed nerve endings, distilling the anger. He wouldn't open the bottles. Not tonight. He'd have the security of knowing they were in his press, behind a locked front door. Not a time bomb – he'd always been able to do this. Tomorrow. Wait till tomorrow. He had just one last task to do. The label.

* * * *

Next morning, Ronnie was first in, placing the label nearly in front of his model before making his excuses, dodging Martin's questioning look, muttering that he'd be back later. He later learned that the media had arrived before the civic dignitaries and their visitors; the showcase had been judged a triumph; touring it had been mooted, the practicalities to be discussed later. The participants had soon tired of the mocktails as lurid as Herself's silk wrappings and, led by The Artist formerly Known as Dinny, had reclaimed their miscellaneous alcoholic booty from the safe and headed for the embankment. It was a balmy June day, after all, and fuck the civic visitors. It was their city, too – right?

Ronnie learned later that the visitors had been puzzled by the title of his piece – *Futility* – and after a short debate, deemed it an astute social comment on post-Covid society.

Everyone had been baffled at how, after the visitors had gone and before lock-up, the model masterpiece had somehow collapsed into a heap of thousands of little matchsticks. Had the glue been defective? Surely Ronnie could rebuild it to its former glory. He could start next time he came in?

Only Maggie had remained when Ronnie had slipped back into the centre. She'd been busy in the office, preparing to lock up. She hadn't seen him quietly crushing the fragile walls, pushing in the delicate roof. It only took a couple of minutes, and he was gone.

* * * *

Walking home. Ronnie knew would never be back to rebuild, never again set foot in the centre with its dismal indignity of mindless activity and inane conversation. He was glad they'd be warm for the winter. He wished Martin well. It had served him for a while, he supposed. It had put in a couple of years, got the social services and his GP off his back. He was seen to be *Making an Effort*. Enough, though. It was over. He was ready for the next phase of his existence. And he smiled to himself and increased his pace, thinking of the two litre bottles of Powers waiting in his press at home.

The Dead Who Kill the Living

Eddie is alone as he sets off on his walk after 11 mass at St. Patrick's every Sunday. The comfort of routine. Calling into Bradley's for a paper and a takeaway tea, just a dash of milk, no sugar. Rolling tobacco and papers. A nod, an exchange of the day's news – who's dead, who's in hospital, the weather, the football. No reciprocal questions about how it's going, his family. They all know. Then driving the couple of miles round tortuous narrow bends into the hills, where there are few signposts and fewer signs of human habitation. He pulls in at the side of the road, under the trees, just yards from the entrance to the cemetery. He stands at the gate, drinks his tea, rolls a few cigarettes for the walk. Zips up his hoodie and sets off on the path on the opposite side of the road.

The others, he knows, will join him on the way, as he follows the myriad of twisting, unstable paths up the wind torn hillside, deep into the forest. A sensory presence so close at times he imagines he can hear their voices from the void, feel imagined touches of hands long gone, catch the echo of remembered footsteps.

He is older now; some would say old. His travelling companions, forever young.

This is a place of remembering.

Perhaps one elusive day of forgetting.

He dares not believe so.
It is not his time. Yet.
For now, he walks.

* * * *

There was a winter when he had walked almost every night, head bowed against lashing rain, slipping and sliding on the churned mud underfoot. Clutching for purchase on the slippery moss of tree trunks to steady himself, picking his way through mulched leaves and the tangled scatology of undergrowth. Sodden trainers, the Arctic wind cutting through his thin parka, numbing muscle and bone but not his mind, the watery beam of his pocket torch circling the forest floor. It was his penance.

That was back in the late nineties. He'd been home for a few years, his world expanding little beyond the four walls of his Ma's old house, when the word came to him, from young men he did not know, emissaries of old men he had once known as brothers.

The war was over. The bodies had to be found. Given a Christian burial. There was a Commission being set up.

Only no one knew exactly where they were, the unmarked graves.

Dug frantically in the small hours by frightened teenagers, unfamiliar with a spade. Filled in, in a panic, covered over, left to the elements.

Unreliable memories occluded by time and alcohol and Diazepam, mental breakdown and death.

They had been the local knowledge. The boys on the ground. Knowing only what they needed to know. That was the way of it.

Long inactive, they were depending on him.

What were the chances, after twenty-five odd years, of some cathartic recognition of a suddenly familiar twist or turn?

When all he remembered was the deep darkness, the Belfast voices with their hard vowels cursing at them to dig faster, for fuck's sake, the cold sweat soaking his jumper. Brogan fumbling for a light as they huddled under a tree, sharing a fag. The fear of what he might hear or see and dare not think about. The single shot.

* * * *

Early in the new century, the Forestry had moved in with their diggers. Planting an abundance of young fir trees to swell and renew the indigenous forest. What might they accidentally uncover? Cross-border EU funding for a new Ireland of tourism and leisure. Bilingual signage. Boards describing the area's ancient history, its plant and bird life. Kids on youth employment schemes installing flat pack picnic benches and tables. Pensioners in Men's Sheds crafting bird and book boxes.

Those firs were tall now.

At weekends, a pop-up coffee shack fashioned from a disused horsebox, where disinterested, lithe teenage girls in leggings and sweatshirts dispensed frothy barista oat milk cappuccinos at nearly twice the going rate.

Would we ever have thought it, he would imagine saying to Brogan. Me *reared on tea, drinking fancy coffee at nearly four quid a time. Our Mammys would be turning in their grave.*

Always here, the word. Graves.

* * * *

They had been so young. All of them. But youth was no defence.

It was Brogan who had collected the car, left unlocked outside a pub in the Main Street. Probably, he knew later, by arrangement. Taken in plain sight. Hot-wired it, and away up the road to the border before anyone looked sideways at them. Not that there'd have been much resistance. Sure wouldn't the owners have a claim? It was a banger, anyway.

Shouldn't be drinking and driving anyway, feck them, Brogan had laughed derisively, adrenaline coursing through his veins, pushing it to seventy on the narrow tortuous roads. *Doing them a good turn. Good Samaritans, that's us, Eddie lad.* No lights, no signposts. No licence, no fear.

They criss-crossed the border, pulling up at the arranged rendezvous spot on the edge of the forest. Lights off. Chain smoking Sweet Afton, spluttering as the inhaled harshness tore their throat. The silence broken only by Brogan's random bursts of bravado, of self-justification.

The fucker had it coming to him.

What could have been going through the young man's mind, he wondered, trussed and gagged in a car boot, bruised and broken, rancid with urine and faeces, cloying blood and stale sweat, all that long road from his native Belfast to unknown borderlands? Knowing he was never coming back? Had he been so weary, had the pain been so severe that there was a sense of resignation, of longing for the bullet that would end it all?

Sensing his disquiet, Brogan elbowed him sharply.

Calm yourself. Orders is orders. We're only doing what we're bid.

The shovels had been taken from a sympathetic local farmer's outhouse and hidden there a couple of days before. No one came walking round these parts back then. They burned inside the car, just over the border. Then the tramp to the outhouse where they were to spend the night. The ache in his guts, the exhaustion. Sleepless.

"Get to sleep and this time tomorrow we'll be drinking our full in Blaney. Yes, lad!"

Brogan had slapped him on the back, Brogan had drunk his fill the next night, true enough, and for many and any nights he could get his hands on it, until the craving for alcohol and the need for oblivion took him too down a lonely, frightened path to a bullet in the brain.

* * * *

There were other reasons to keep up the walking, of course.

The counsellor he had finally agreed to see after his last spell in hospital had recommended regular physical exercise. So had his young GP once he hit his fifties. Skinny as ever, his cholesterol was still too high, his blood pressure marginal. Heart attack. Stroke. *Sniper's alley* they call that decade. The irony.

Anything that took him out of the wee terraced house gave him a routine, a purpose. Fresh air. Feel-good endorphins.

Aye, right?

But how could they understand these children of the Ceasefire for all their professional qualifications? How could they grasp that wherever you walked, the past walked with you? And when you tried to put your head down to sleep, its voices whispered their way in and stayed through the long hours before dawn?

Recently, he had felt, the boundaries between worlds had got thinner, the dead speaking to him more clearly than the living.

He has told the priest this.

The priest, far from his land of birth, struggling with the local dialect, had looked at him, smiling in indulgent incomprehension.

He still attended regularly. Apart from Palm Sunday.

His Mammy had loved Palm Sunday. The annual emotive rendering of *The Holy City*.

The families of the Disappeared had taken to holding vigils then. Their haunted faces calling for the information that would allow them to retrieve the remains of their loved ones, before it was too late, before all those who knew were themselves gone. Time was running out. They begged for closure.

So did he. Every day.

Still he walked.

* * * *

He was not the only one.

Through therapy and group work, he had met so many broken

souls. People who would have killed each other in their youth, sharing their suffering.

The woman who sleep walked the floor, washing remembered blood off the walls.

The man who couldn't deal with goods packed in polystyrene after handling corpses covered in tiny white balls of melting chemicals after an explosion at an electrical goods shop

How every townland, every place of worship resonated not with beauty but with remembered death and funeral rites, the landscape and topography of the country forever skewed

The mothers spending their nights in graveyards to keep their sons company. Spreading blankets to make sure their boys were warm beneath the cold earth. Lighting candles for youngsters afraid of the dark.

All failing to cope in their own way, all going through the mechanics of living

All waiting for it to end.

* * * *

A crepuscular sky, a chill wind soughing the pines. He would go home soon

The sisters had long since given up calling on a Sunday evening to see if he was all right. They knew he was what he was. They accepted.

He was proud of his nieces and nephews, he loved them, but he found their world so unfamiliar and often he was too tired to pretend.

The same sisters had long since given up hoping he'd meet someone and settle down.

A bit late in the day to be taking on another fellow traveller.

How could anyone understand?

Brogan's young wife had gone back to her Ma's in Dundalk about it, unable to cope with the night terrors, the tremors, the black moods where relief could not be found at the bottom of a bottle however often he tried.

That was one thing. At least the drink had never got him.

Nor the pills.

He'd taken them in the past.

As his GP said, he knew they were there if he ever needed them, temporarily.

A cup of tea would do fine. Leaf through the paper, not that there was much in them nowadays.

Maybe a bit of telly, but what was there to watch on a Sunday night?

Better to sit in the twilight, lost in a past that was so much more vivid than the present. Until the voices got too loud.

He'd been feeling exhausted lately. Worn out. Not much appetite – less than usual. He didn't think he'd bother the doctor about it. Back in the day, he'd never imagined seeing out his three score years and ten.

There couldn't be long to go now.

Sleep might come, as he waited for the big sleep. Who would be there to meet him?

Brogan?

He smiled at the thought.

If he was lucky, blessed oblivion.

For now, he was forever imprisoned by this land where, it seemed to him, as he walked to his car in the gathering dusk, it is the dead who kill the living.

No Goodbyes

The brown sauce decides it for me. I can't go to the supermarket any more. It's stupid. I keep putting the things he loved in the basket. Like the dearest brown sauce. I always got it for him, dear and all, even when I told him it was a waste of money, they all taste the same. I'll be walking along the aisles, on autopilot, and next thing I see it in the basket. I don't remember picking it up, but there it is.

I don't need it now.

Hoodies, too. Grey hoodies. They're a trigger. I'll be going along minding my own business and out of the corner of my eye I'll see some young fella in a light grey hoodie and for that split second I think *Aaron.* My feet taking me towards him, his name in my mouth. Then I remember.

It's not just me.

There are so many of us out there. Too many. Mothers. I know that now. The doctor got me to join a support group, go to counselling. I didn't want to; what was the point? It wouldn't bring Aaron back. I'm a private sort of person,. I'm not one for airing my business in public. My grief's my privilege for loving him, not something to put all over social media.

What is there to say? You have a son who can't get work, always short of money, but he has his family, out and about with his mates, full of craic – until one day he's not.

I've learned a lot since Aaron.

Sometimes, the pain lies dormant, buried for years, from a childhood when you just couldn't deal with it, so you blanked it out.

This one man I met had been a victim of childhood abuse; sexual stuff. One day he read a report about it in the paper and something struck a chord in him. He recognised the name of the school, the teacher. Next thing he remembers is waking up in mental hospital. The police found him on the bridge, ready to jump. He doesn't remember going there. He doesn't remember anything about it.

I'll be forever looking for answers.

One mother I met has buried two of her sons. The first one was on drugs. They found him at the house where he'd been living. Pure yellow, he was. It took him three days to die. She agreed to switch off the life support system. She thinks she's a murderer. Her younger boy couldn't cope. He wanted to be with his brother. She couldn't stop him. No drugs this time. She says he was as perfect on the inside as he was on the outside when they found him. How do you cope with that?

Another mother I got talking to says her life's on rewind, looking for the signs she missed. She can't forgive herself. Her boy was so affectionate. He always had a hug and a kiss for her. Looking back now, she can remember when he stopped hugging her. Was that a sign, she asks? On Mother's Day, he bought her a big Easter egg. He was gone by Easter. Was that a warning, too? *I should have noticed,* she says. *I should have noticed the little things.* Might she have changed anything?

You meet so many good people when you get involved in groups and stuff. There was this young woman, I'll never forget her, three wee wins. She told us she went to the cemetery every day for months, to scream her anger at her man's grave. Her husband took his life and left her to rear them. Why?

My son, my Aaron, he was always away from the house at the weekends, with his friends. So when we hadn't heard from him for a few days, nobody thought anything was wrong. But I knew. Here in my gut. A mother knows. I carried him in my womb for nine months. I carried him when he couldn't walk. When he was sick. I carried his coffin. He was twenty. A mother shouldn't have to do that. You never think that'll happen. Ever. It's not the natural order of things. I tell myself he's in a better life now. I have to. But I don't understand why.

I miss him so much.

It's not logical. Even when a child dies in a road accident or from an illness, there's a reason. You can talk it through, and explain it. You have answers to the questions. With a suicide, the dead leave the questions for you.

I see him in the garage. What was he thinking as he stood there, that he'd never see us again? Or was the pain so great that he didn't think anything except to end it?

I heard people screaming at me not to go in, but he was my son, my child. I had to get to him. His brother cut him down. I had to hug him, to rub his cold hands to try to warm them. I was screaming for an ambulance. But I knew he was dead. I was sobbing on my hands and knees in the middle of the road. I couldn't stop. Nothing got to me until my mother called to me to come away and I let her lead me to the house.

Sometimes, when I wake up, I forget for that first split of a second that Aaron's dead. Then I remember.

The family's split, since. His brother can't have his name mentioned. Can't talk about it. Can't look at his photo. Others talk about it all the time. The week before he died, his sister shouted at him to stop drinking. She was only trying to help. But she feels guilty now. His god-daughter's three. She can't understand. She loves humming a song about suicide that she hears on the radio. What can we say to her? We're walking on eggshells round each other. It's hard, meeting face to face.

His friends came to the house at the start. There were hundreds of tributes on the social media sites. Wee poems, pictures of flickering candles, *forever young*. I wanted to shout at them, *Where were you when he was sitting in the house, with nothing to do?* You only ever rang him the day he got his benefit, to go for a drink. *Come on up the banking, we've a few cans*. Weekends, dole money. Drink. It's a party thing. Friends equals drink equals friends. There's a blind acceptance of it in our society. And drugs. Prescription drugs don't even get counted in suicide reports, they don't even record if they found them in the body, because they're not classed as illegal. Don't tell me they don't have an effect.

I know I'll only see Aaron again when I'm dead, and it's like an explosion in the heart. I want to go to him but I couldn't do it. I can't. Suicide. I've seen what it does to those left behind. I'm terrified his friends don't see that. Once it happens in a group, it becomes an option. Another follows.

I think, to myself, if he had known how much people cared…. But you don't have to die to realise that. You don't. Believe me. There's nothing cool about a six-foot coffin. It's cold. Very, very cold.

Nobody Tramps on My Dahlias

A feisty nanny goat inspired it, though I would be teenage-curious before I troubled to find out. Forgiven when she lunched on the dangling garments pegged to the washing line, indulged when she munched on the brim of an unwelcome caller's straw boater, trampling a cherished flower bed was a hoof too far. My four-year-old mother watched in awe as her diminutive granny physically hauled the errant Biddy to the garden shed and shackled her. Exclaiming with what breath she had to spare from what was undoubtedly a significant physical exertion for a five-foot septuagenarian, that *nobody tramped on her dahlias*. Thus was a boundary of unacceptable behaviour defined in generational hearth language.

It was a phrase that would punctuate with pride your protracted journey away from us. For while the cruelty that is Alzheimer's robbed you of so much, it never took your dignity, your sense of humour, your wonderful smile that lights our path as we are still learning how to live without you.

* * * *

I go looking for you in the ladies' toilets. The cubicle door is open, pools of urine, crumples of paper on the floor. You are gripping a basin, motionless, both taps gushing down the plughole, staring into the mirror above it. What do you see there? Not me. Not you. Not today.

An ominous chill seeps from my core. The echo of random irrationalities. I wasn't ready. Glossy MDF panelling, cream porcelain with wildflower stencilling, garish faux dressing room lighting. The pungency of heavy floral air freshener. In that most ignominious of settings, we had begun our long goodbye.

I straighten your skirt and guide you back to where we are cosy in a window seat of the small, family-run hotel. Concentrated eye contact, urging the others to make small talk, order more coffee, anything to engage you while I make my excuses back to mop, wipe and flush.

You are genetically proud. Dignified.

You hadn't noticed.

My daughter, uneasy, follows me out, puts her head round the bathroom door.

"What are you doing?"

"Nothing. Just – sorting myself. I wanted to get granny back to sit down before I fixed my face."

She has always known a lie.

But it is her graduation tomorrow and her beloved Granny here from Ireland to see what she scarcely dared to hope for, become reality. Nothing must spoil this for her.

Maybe granny has a chill, I lie to my unbelieving self.

Later, we leave you in your room to get ready for the gala dinner. The red dress you delight in spread on your bed, your necklace and makeup ready in front of the mirror. Sandals. I know better than to try to downsize your capacious handbag.

Half an hour later I find you sitting on the bed, in your slip.

There is a hole in your new dress, you tell me, accusingly. A big one. You have nothing to wear. We must go without you.

I check. There isn't.

I pull it over your head, zip it up, bend to buckle on the sandals, forget the necklace, pile the makeup into the overflowing bag and hurry you out the door to the car park.

We are tight for time.

You are by nature embarrassingly early.

I hold your hand in the back. I see gratitude and humility at not being left behind. It hurts.

The evening is wonderful. I am too vigilant. We leave early, as planned. Perhaps it's the unfamiliar surroundings, tiredness, excitement that are disorientating you.

Once home, all will be well.

* * * *

The calls become more frequent. More illogical.

There is a power cut – not infrequent in rural Ireland – and the phones are down.

The electricity is weak.

What do you mean?

"There's not enough coming through to cook with. It's the weather."

The microwave is broken.

The range isn't lighting.

The phone isn't working. It must be the electricity supply.

The laptop – unused since my Da's death – is mysteriously switching on and off.

There is a cartoon man on a desert island on the screen.

The radio isn't working. It's playing *some awful music. The tune the old cow died to.*

A neighbour tapes the dial in place on "the news" for you. It still isn't working.

The mobile phone is broken.

I ring each evening, for an hour, to talk about everything and nothing.

Then I ring twice a day.

We visit every few weeks, the long round trip. You will not move.

Can I give up everything and go to live with you? You are fiercely independent. You won't entertain it. I don't want you to. I am too selfish. But I am frightened.

Your neighbours change.

Pleasant, young, indigent.

They don't know you, or even "of" you.

Are you just another invisible old woman with an ever-present smile?

You leave work. You have to.

They buy you a wonderful holiday.

My daughter and her boyfriend travel with you.

She comes back from a week placating and humouring a cantankerous, needy, negative stranger who is everything you are not.

You have gifts for me. It's the family tradition. Spending your holiday money on those at home. Silver earrings. A plastic purse with a picture of kittens. My daughter tells me she demanded Granny buy the earrings she chose for me. Granny insisted on buying the purse.

"It's like you are about seven."

It is cheap, tacky and – for a child.

* * * *

Winter.

We visit one day to find you have no heat.

The fridge is crammed with food. Out of date. Unidentified leftovers in margarine tubs. I clear it out.

A phone call tells of a flat tyre. Then another.

You are alone, and frightened, in a ditch at the side of an isolated border road.

"Why didn't you ring me?"

Of course. The mobile is not working.

There is an accident in a car park. The police are involved. Details are vague, establishing facts provokes anger.

You are not ready to leave this rented house that you and my da made into your home. He is alive – you are alive – in the rickety shelves stuffed with books, the piles of random papers, letters, records, photos, memorabilia piled on every table, spare chair, windowsill, sideboard, dresser. Why would you label them, or put them in order? You know who and what they are, and when you no longer do, it will not matter.

* * * *

The call comes.

Casual, but steely determination in every word.

"I think I'd like you to look for a house somewhere near you. Before the winter. The range isn't working."

What did it cost you to say those words? To ask for help?

I find one, two doors away from me. I pay over the odds in a bidding war against what I suspect may be a phantom buyer.

I pay over the odds to ensure the sitting tenants, who refuse to go, will leave on reasonable terms.

I pay over the odds to have it cleaned and decorated in a style as similar as possible to *home*.

Your landlord, a lifelong friend keen to get out of property, is palpably relieved that you are moving to a safer place. He promises he will not sell the house until he knows you are settled. Just in case.

But I know you. You burn bridges.

We spend two days packing what we can into the removal van. We pay over the odds for extra help, extra storage.

I am making huge decisions on your behalf, and I have no one to ask for guidance. You just want to go. We leave a shed piled full of wood, old ironware, plastic, bags, boxes, newspapers, rags and general detritus from half a century of hoarding. Rooms strewn with books and pamphlets that we cannot possibly accommodate. I fool myself that the charity I have contacted will come for them. It doesn't. You turn the key in the lock and walk away from fifty years of married life for ever. Your strength confounds me. I am weeping. There will be no last goodbyes. We drive down the hill. You don't look back. Not once.

* * * *

City life tries to work.

We plant cuttings from your garden. I have already chosen décor to make it look as much like home as possible. Forty-year-old wallpaper cannot be replicated.

You have brought three feral kittens which were born in your yard and, you tell me, abandoned by their mother while their father keeps a distanced eye over them. *He's a good old boy.* The metaphor of your own childhood is cruel.

We try classes, courses, day centres but they never were and never will be you.

"I am not playing bingo."

The highlight becomes our Saturday morning supermarket trip to buy treats for a family you no longer have and entertaining you will never do. Your presses fill up, just as they did at *home.*

You start to burn things.

One day I find you wearing several T-shirts on top of each other.

"I was cold."

There are cardigans to hand.

You lose things.

I write countless notes.

You lose them too.

We register you with the local health centre. The practice nurse tells us your vital organs are those of a younger woman. She says you could live to ninety-six, a random figure? You like her. She refers us.

The mental health consultant asks questions and I hear you tell him, with authority, that you have no grandchildren. You have no idea of the date, season, year. You don't know who President Kennedy was, so *he can't have been important.* You cannot remember a sequence of three words.

He tells us you have Alzheimer's and gives us booklets. They vanish, overnight.

'If you say so,' your irritated response.

I know so.

Are you frightened, Mammy? I am.

We are becoming lost in separate worlds. How can I stay with you?

I learn never to argue, to contradict, to expect; to intervene only when necessary. You leave taps on. The cooker. I find the cats eating dainty sandwich and bun picnics while you forget to eat. Everything isn't working. I notice one day there isn't a glass or cup that hasn't a chip or crack.

You fall. We get a body alarm, a special phone, a walking aid. Within weeks, each becomes too challenging; we pass it down the hierarchy of need. It's like children's learning toys, once outgrown, only in reverse.

You fall outside the house. In a shop. You keep falling. We move you downstairs, barricade the stairs, and you somehow climb over to get to where your bed used to be. The ambulance men are so good, so kind. There is no point in taking you to hospital, they say. The carers try. We try.

You think I am your mother. The mother you barely knew. After that I sense, arch bluffer that you are, that you confuse my daughter and me.

There is little sleep. I am not the thirty-year-old mother of a baby; I am the sixty-something mother of my mother and we are both exhausted. A social worker insists on respite. You beg me to take you home. We try again but you are admitted late one Eleventh of July night. I circumnavigate unfamiliar territory past road blocks, teetering blazing bonfires, bandsmen who have dispensed with stifling uniform jackets, hats and instruments to drink cans of lager outside crowded pubs.

You do not look back as I close another door for the last time.

Do you know?

We are lucky, I gabble, to have found a care home only a short drive away.

Driving home, it doesn't feel it.

Everyone says you won't last a month.

That you'll give up.

Everyone is wrong.

You last three and a half years.

* * * *

My daughter visits. She cannot stop the tears. Granny is gone and a smiling travesty remains, tea stains on a synthetic pink cardigan she would never have chosen, hair cut in an institutional bob, nodding silently in response to everything. Always smiling.

"When it's your turn, Ma – Switzerland," she mutters.

But there are hugs, interactions, coffee drunk in companionable silence leafing through old photo books, to bring unexpected light to this relentless, interminably slow decomposition of body and mind.

The first alert comes the next spring after an infection when you do not know me, know anyone.

"What do you see?" asks the doctor, gently.

"I see a very elderly woman who has had a long and wonderfully full life coming to the end."

I do not recognise my voice.

The carers feed you ice cream, soft chocolate, frothy coffees, everything you love. You abandon dinners, drink sherry.

You are happiest in the company of men, I tell them. They assign you male nurses.

"Do you know who I am, Mammy?" I ask one day.

The nurses are listening.

And one last, precious time, you affirm the dear name you chose for me. My heart swells as I squeeze your fragile hand too tightly.

It's the last cognisant thing you say.

Soon, you will be voiceless. You have no more need for words.

I focus myself to finish an imagined memoir I have been working on, about my Da's childhood. I bring you the first copy. Rituals. I slowly turn the pages.

Every time his photo appears – as a child, as the young RAF navigator, you smile. That wonderful smile. You know him. I included the pen pal picture you sent him, a vibrant, very beautiful teenager, poised beyond your years. How young you were – Fourteen? fifteen?

Suddenly I realise how foolish we are. That, of course, you have not recognised the old man of Da's last years from my photo books.

You have been looking for the man you fell in love with. The young, passionately intense, tireless airman. It is him you have been waiting for.

* * * *

You, the great survivor, survive.

One afternoon, a nurse rings me to say she detects a change.

Do I want Mammy admitted to hospital for observation?

I know what she would say.

When I enter your room, I know what the nurse means. Our eyes meet.

You are leaving.

Hearing is the last sense to go, so I hold your hand, moisten your lips and talk to you through the evening. Time suspends. The universe centres on your small, simple room. There is nothing more to say. No regrets. It has all been said.

I read your favourite Psalm. Or is it mine?

Your faith is strong, your cynicism about organised religion a mark of the woman you are.

When it's your time, you told me with the quiet assurance of one who knows, your da will come for me.

The nurse makes me a coffee. I take it to the door, breathe in the frosty December air. The clear night sky sparkles with stars.

I am sent home to pack for the vigil.

It won't be tonight.

I am wakened from an unexpected deep sleep by the phone. I drive recklessly through swirling fog, down dimly lit roads. Unseen hands hold open the door for me.

I race upstairs.

They will say I just made it.

But you are gone.

You have been gone for a very long time.

I bend to kiss your still-warm face. You are smiling.

* * * *

There are no funerals on Christmas Day. We spend it in limbo, at my daughter's, another empty seat at our small family table. I bring all the photo albums. We eat mince slices made from your recipe, though not to your standard, drink endless coffees, reminisce, attempt a massive crossword in your memory.

We cannot know it, but there will be an extra seat at the table next Christmas. A sling, for my two-week-old grandson, born of life's longing for itself. I will be Granny. And when he blesses us with his first smiles, it will be the face of my Da, your *anam cara*, smiling at me.

On St. Stephen's Day we take you on your last journey to the windswept border hillside where you will join my Da. Your flowers a blaze of red, like your last outfit – the wonderful red dress from graduation. I speak as I do best – from a scatter of notes, from the heart.

Afterwards, I stop to buy a takeaway coffee from your local shop.

You won. You made it.

Bizarre, this thought that comes unbidden.
Maybe you did.
No one ever tramped on your dahlias.

Collateral Damage

They burst from the bright red Renault with the 'R' plates, upbeat as the music blaring from the speakers, animated, laughing. The girl throws her school-bag into the back and lifts two giant-sized takeaway cups from the console. She snatches off the lids to reveal an indulgence of whipped cream, chocolate shards, mini marshmallows, dribbled with sauce. Is there room for a drink underneath this confection?

How old is she? Sixteen? The box-pleated school skirt looks incongruously childish, her tie already loosened, shirt collar undone, sleeves rolled up. He, maybe a year or two older. T-shirt, tracksuit bottoms. Study day? Already left school? A cloudless blue sky over bleached grass. Exam weather. The girl glances at her watch, tosses her blonde ponytail, whispers, giggles, and, gulping their drinks, they scamper off towards the river. They are oblivious to the elderly woman in the blue Fiesta parked in the opposite corner. They are oblivious to everything except themselves and the joy of escape on this glorious June day.

Early, the woman is always early. She cannot stay beyond noon. The fragile, balancing act of her life demands it. He will be late. She hopes he won't text unnecessary apologies when he's stopped at the lights, foolishly risking penalty points. She has his shopping in a bag on the passenger seat: a voucher for phone credit, postage stamps, ready meals, supermarket own-brand brandy. The shopping that means he can spend his respite hour with her.

Just after half past ten on a Thursday, the rest of the car park empty, the play park childless. Such a banal setting for their weekly rendezvous.

The passenger door opens, and he flops into the seat beside her, out of breath, prising his mobile from his back pocket to set it on the dashboard. He mustn't miss a call. They exchange carrier bags, and thanks. It's a routine, the small courtesies surviving.

"You're awful good. Really, thanks."

She accepts the twenty-pound note; otherwise, he won't ask again and their meeting will be even shorter.

"Couple of books you might like. Let me know what you think of them, Take your time, I'm in no hurry for them back. I got a good haul in the charity shop last Friday."

Both of them with an indulgence of reading time now and no one to share it with. By their age, you're either a reader or you're not.

"Will we go for a walk?"

It's rhetorical. He is already getting out. Walk and talk, that's what they do.

She picks up her bag with the flask and mug, locks the car.

He is heading in their usual direction. She reaches for his arm to stop him.

"Maybe we could go this way today?" He raises his eyebrows, quizzical. Their paths are as familiar as themselves.

"Just before you arrived –"

"I'm sorry I was late, I couldn't get away.. It must have been ten past when the girl got to us. Another new one. Carers don't stick it long, but can you blame them?"

She shushes him.

"You're here. No, it's that, just before you arrived, this young couple drove in. They were obviously in a hurry. It looked like she'd just got out of an exam. Still in her school uniform. They went that way."

She gestures towards the river, knowingly.

"Let's give them a bit of space."

"Lucky them," he smiles.

There is a brief silence, then, arms linked, they walk on, heading to the right towards the little wood. There are benches and picnic tables there, she reminds him. They can sit and talk in comfort. Which, of course, is what they do. Once a week, for a snatched meeting, all the trivia of home life jumbled with their thoughts on global politics, the cost-of-living crisis, what they've seen, and listened to, and read. The solvent of his dear familiar presence soothes away her tensions, the knots in her spine fluid, her head flopped against the familiar comfort of his shoulder..

"I could sleep," she smiles,

"Go ahead."

But of course she cannot. It is enough to indulge in this reminder of what they were, too briefly. What she chooses to believe they still are, at some unspoken and intangible level.

What she used to fancy they might be again in the future. She has watched powerless while the future became the present, then the past.

Sentences trip over each other as they sip their coffee. So much to say. None of it important. For everything that matters has already been said. How can this simple act encompass such intimacy? They are together. The extraneous is irrelevant.

Just as she has been determined, as she has been so many times, to consign this snatched ritual to history, to dismiss it as just another routine in a week defined by routines, she feels herself melting into this unfathomably deep stillness of belonging. Of coming home.

It is not home, of course. But it is where she can rest.

Nearly forty years ago, now. They'd been driven by some compulsion beyond their rational selves, any sense of consequence. She, at least, had always known they must come back, but she would never, never regret running headlong towards that magical glimpse of freedom.

In the comfortable stillness, they share indulgent stories about grandchildren. They smile over pictures on their phones. It is as near as they get to mentioning the future. The jokes about side by side in the same care home stopped being funny years ago.

Occasionally, and less so, now, they may reminisce.

The best week of their life. Walking the narrow streets of the Dam late at night, wrapped in each other's arms; fantasy window shopping – calculating and recalculating the unbelievable price of a black lace dress; watching with admiration a craftworker deftly fashioning a violin in the front window of his artisan studio. A picnic of warm crusty bread, creamy Gouda cheese and spicy sausage in the Vondelpark; the Rijksmuseum, a Stendhal of emotions, he smiling indulgently as her tears fell unbidden as she stood transfixed before the unfathomable magnificence of Starry Night. She avowed it the most peaceful place she had ever been, but perhaps the peace had been within her. The coffee shop where, despite much teasing, they favoured brandies over smoking and became new regulars. The charming couple who introduced themselves with the words, *You must be honeymooners*, and told the simple story of their own enduring love in this most inclusive city of culture. Teetering on unstable heels over rickety boardwalks in the flower market to buy bulbs that withered in their carrier bag. The afternoon of the thunderstorm when they lay in bed, made love, drank too much beer, talked and dozed and held each other and later, hurling the glasses into the Amstel with the abandonment of total irresponsibility and the promise to return.

They never did. They no longer mention it.

When, she wonders, did reminiscence supplant dreaming? Was it a gradual process? Try as she might, she cannot think of one defining moment, one pivotal event. Like most things, it evolved organically.

"Happy?"

She nods.

"Peaceful? Me too. My soul rests in you," he adds, quietly, and she wonders what it has cost him to say it.

Neither wants to be seen checking a watch, but they know only too well how quickly time passes when they are engrossed in each other. By unspoken consent, they get up, empty the dregs of the coffee into the grass. She puts the flask into her bag and they turn back towards the car.

She sees him wincing. Do his legs ache now as well as his back?

"That wasn't too far for you?"

For a moment, he isn't sure if she is teasing or in earnest.

"I'm a lot better this week."

"It could be stress. You underestimate the pressure you're under. Full-time caring isn't easy."

Especially caring for someone who is...*challenging* is the accepted term.

He yawns.

"Bored?" she teases.

He gently cuffs her shoulder.

"Less of your cheek. I got two, maybe three hours last night."

"He sleeps like the dead."

An unfortunate turn of phrase, but one that trips so readily off the tongue she doesn't bother to correct it.

"I have it easy," she adds.

They arrive at the car park in time to see the youngsters, laughing, dishevelled, piling back into their car and driving off with a screech of tyres and a blast of hip-hop.

Time is up for them all.

They hold each other. *Tender, she thinks, it is tender.* She is far from suppressed longing or frustrated passion. She prays for the day when she may be blessed with the gift of indifference.

She pulls away.

"On you go. You'll be late. I'll text you later."

"Next Thursday?"

"Of course."

She smiles.

And so it will be, every Thursday until the carers' service is cut. Or one of them goes into residential care. Or dies. They are all old now.

Or until she can rationalise whether she had been seduced by the beauty of the city, the welcome of blue skies and sunshine, the sheer daring of kicking over the traces of an ordered life to shelve her responsibilities, and to hell with the consequences, to be self-indulgent, hedonistic, to – as she'd seen it them – to really *live?*

Surely life is the weekly routine, the compromise, the banality of doing the right thing. She has to believe that.

Selfish – you're so selfish, she tells herself. She has good female friends, a quiet home, the joy of grandchildren. *Much to be grateful for.* The hollow phrase, never enough to quash the inner wish for more. And she will never quell it while they maintain this tired ritual.

Suddenly, she is resolute. Why have they have bound themselves to it? What need compels her? Her rational self says it is futile, a trite mockery of of who and what they once thought they were.. Why does she continue to let it define her week? There is irrevocable insecurity yet also great strength in the courage to let go.

She can post back the books. She need never do his shopping again. Next week, next Thursday, she will not come. She will hurt him, but only she is strong enough to free them both from clinging to inequitable hope. It is too late. It has been too late for a very long time.

They will be safer with memories. Of that indulgent, wonderful week that they can never allow themselves to atone for. They had caused immense hurt. They had come home, as she knew they would. But there are some things you cannot come home to, because they were never there in the first place.

Yet, she smiles as she thinks of the young couple. Do the ponytailed girl's parents know about the boy? Do the boy's parents know he has borrowed the car? Has she been missed at school? Will it be worth it for that stolen time?

"Yes," she hears herself saying to the empty car, "yes and yes."

She is suddenly overwhelmed by an impulse to try to find them, to shout at them that routine will always be there but the youthful vibrancy of their passion will not. That time will distil it, they will grow, most probably grow apart. She wants to make them realise these are the precious moments of untempered joy that elevate life from its tedious banality. Go with it. Have no regrets.

For she has none.

Duty and guilt drive her to live a lie as surely as she had known they would, the moment when the plane had touched down on an inescapably grey and rainy Belfast, and they had gripped each other's hands to face, separately, the return to reality. Everything has a price. And you keep on paying. She had known, then, soul deep, that the two of them are, and always would be, the heart's collateral damage.

Letter to My Younger Self

Hello you.

You visited me the other day.

I was cleaning up a little wooden cabinet, wondering if it'd be suitable for my grandson, whose ecologically conscious parents have asked for no plastic toys, please. You remember it. About a foot tall, with five drawers, each a different bright colour, with varnished knobs and a scattering of flowers painted around the borders. I think it may have been a sewing box as there's a wooden post on the top to hold a spool of thread – or, as my story books described it, *a reel of cotton.* It never did. It was our treasure chest, custodian of secrets. Things to be kept for our future. That's me. I'm the future. How strange that sounds.

You visited me in the form of scribbled notes on a page torn from a school jotter what was lodged at the back of the cobalt blue drawer. *'Books I am going to write.'* Even then, the writing is almost illegible, another device to keep it secret should any adult happen upon it. I can decipher it. Because I remember.

Writing was the guilty secret that carried you through the other one, the one imposed on you through no fault of your own; the one that had you self-harming, cutting your feet, and picking at your nails until they bled, long before you knew what the verb implied. That sustained you through the medicated early teenage years, trapped in an unwelcome body marked with acne, boils and nervous rashes, distorted by the weaponry of food, yearning to escape. Always writing.

I want to go back and give you the biggest hug ever and tell you, from our future, that it will be all right – much more than all right. But there will be a price to pay, and a lot of healing, which is as much painful as palliative.

You are loved. Valued. It does get better. You will transform yourself. Fight your way out of that unhappy body and emerge, if not like the vacuous, lithe and fawning-eyed beauties of *Jackie* and *Just 17* that you so admire, as a woman who faces her reflection every morning and smiles. You will write. You will make good use of the eidetic memory, that unwelcome echo chamber that haunts you. Look deep – your soul knows that. And others will read it and you will use your words to help others discover the healing power of writing for change. Even the more fatuous dreams – television, news reading, Green rooms, spotlights, they are waiting for you, too. And when you become a mammy yourself, you – we – will find that, until that point, we have never known the all-consuming power of loving and being loved unconditionally. Together, we are healing generational trauma. It ends here.

I wish I could time-travel and take you away, help you heal, comfort you with the whispered assurance of how good life can be. Thirties, forties, fifties, now sixties – it just gets better. Everything starts to make sense. With age comes the freedom to be oneself, to succeed or fail without censure, to cherish the little things which ultimately are the big things. For now, this letter to you, my Younger Self, must suffice. You'll be so glad you didn't give up, on yourself, on your writing, on life. I'm glad that you saved every scrap of that writing. It's been inspirational to your older self – me. Together, we did it.

The characters in Felicity McCall's acutely observed stories walk the earth haunted by the ghosts of the past. The fallout from decades of generational trauma, of alcoholism, depression, loss, is fully evident here. Illness steals memories, addiction ruins lives and so often, it is the women who bear the full brunt when family life implodes. There are no fairy tales here. There is false security in ritual, in routine, in the gamble of the magic roundabout of addiction that keeps on going around, that threatens to throw the player off on that one last spin. Stark and unflinching, empathic, humane, this collection is a celebration of 'the vital pulse of existence', conveyed in a hand that has the lightest, the most sensitive of touches.

Bernie McGill,
2023 Edge Hill Short Story Prize winner and novelist

A sublime collection of stories, humane and poignant, evocative and beautifully written. Present experience triggers memories – good and bad – which are personal to the characters yet universal in their themes: parents and children, loss and trauma, hope and joy. A deeply moving exploration of the weight of the past, the wounds of love and the wonder of human resilience.

Brian McGilloway,
best-selling crime fiction author

Poignant writing, capturing glimpses of the extraordinary in everyday lives.

Sue Divin,
award-winning young adult fiction author

These stories offer insightful reflections on living with the legacy of conflict, trauma and addiction, suffused with warmth, empathy and the joy of acceptance and serenity later life can bring.

Freya McClements,
Northern editor, Irish Times

Uncompromising, honest. Deeply felt emotion underlies these acutely observed and authentic stories. Always compassionate and believable, Felicity McCall walks us unerringly through some of the most telling issues of our time: guilt, the nature of parental love, loss, age related role reversal, the fragmenting impact of suicide, the sly, stubborn power of addiction, the implications of sexual offending, dementia and PTSD. With a strong Northern flavour, and the sure-footedness of a seasoned journalist, she refuses to duck the implications of Northern Ireland's Troubles, in full recognition of inter-generational trauma and the long journey we are on as individuals and society, towards healing. Underlying this writing is the existential challenge of loneliness, the struggle for meaning and human connection, the need for self-actualisation and self-love. Touching, yet avoiding sentimentality, the collection's resolved message has to ultimately be one of hope as embodied in her Letter to my Younger Self in which she perhaps echoes Julian of Norwich, when she says that, the future '…will be all right – much more than all right … even if there is a price to pay, even if the healing is … as much painful as palliative'. All this and more, delivered with an economy of language and a facility to land the killer punch. These are serious straight from the shoulder stories from a serious writer. A writer with something to say.

Jim Simpson,
author and playwright